STARLING DARLING

ERICA VIPOND

MINUET PRESSE

CONTENTS

To eleven year old me, who never guessed, but always hoped, the years of journal keeping would lead to here

PROLOGUE

The night air was a blade sharp against her cheeks as the world whipped past. *Thud thud thud* hunted her. The sidewalks of Amsterdam were slick with rain, but she couldn't afford to stop or slow down.

Since arriving in the city, it'd been impossible to shake a feeling she was being watched. The second her eyes met his, confusion fused with alarm until, at the last possible moment, she'd broken out into a run. She hadn't counted on how fast he was.

As she pushed through obstructing crowds, it was clear they were oblivious to the danger she was in. No one would save her except herself.

A slow burn was alight in her lungs as she took a hasty right turn, quickly calculating what might be her last opportunity to get somewhere safe. Through a blur of bystanders, she glimpsed an opening wide enough to flag an approaching taxi. If she could do that, she might have a chance.

A shop door abruptly flew open, a father and son only noticing her at the last instant. She missed them by millimeters and nearly collided with the glass. A shout of indignation sounded behind her, but she didn't check to confirm if it was *him*. Fear snared like wire around her throat as intensely as her fingers tangled around the strap of her bag.

So much had been taken from her already. She didn't want to lose another thing.

At a vaguely familiar intersection, she expected a shortcut to a different neighborhood. Her shoe landed in a broken crevice of sidewalk full of rainwater, splashing at her ankle. An instant after she went left onto the darkened street, her mistake was evident. Panting, she realized a ten-foot partition blocked a direct way through. Shadows cast forth on the path ahead, an ominous foretelling of what would come if she didn't hurry.

Both hands fumbled on the brick ledge while one leg swung helplessly below. Footsteps echoed closer. The damp air and rain made the climb a slippery and impossible endeavor. Panic mounted, but she kept reaching. Rough hands pulled at her coat, the sky suddenly shrinking.

She fought for balance as her feet stumbled on solid ground. Whirling to face him, she breathed heavily in a gray mist between them. With fists at each side, she steeled herself to fight. He had followed her to a dead end full of garbage and waste.

She was trapped.

Chapter One

New York City, 11 days earlier

The air was filled with the fragrances of May, but not even flowers could soften New York City. Lucia's pace matched the burgeoning traffic as she exited the subway station. Hurrying, she was already twenty minutes late to dinner with Simon. Cherry blossoms rustled overhead as she cut through Washington Square Park, the fountain burbling lightly over cars honking their impatience during rush hour. Corners of the street grew lengthened shadows as afternoon inched toward evening.

Lucia veered south on Sullivan, wavering between resignation and dread. Dinner was in celebration of her thirty-second birthday, but all it did was mark how much time had passed since she'd seen her mother. A small part of her wondered if it would be the birthday her mother finally called. For nearly five years, she'd anticipated it, hoped for it. She'd rehearsed one-sided conversations of what she might say, how gracious she'd be, articulating her regret for her side of the silence. In each scenario, Lucia wondered if she might readily forgive her mother for what had been said that last Christmas if offered enough contrition. There was so much left unspoken between them.

Rounding the corner of West 3rd, Lucia stepped into the restaurant. Her eyes searched for her friend and found him sitting in a booth near the bar.

"Sorry, sorry," said Lucia with a grimace. "I lost track of time working on that Estonia water project I mentioned yesterday."

"It's your birthday. You get a pass," said Simon. He danced a bite of fried artichoke at her on a fork while she took a seat across from him. Lucia snatched it up before he could protest. She reached across the table and squeezed his hand in an affectionate greeting.

"Should I order something, or do I get to be surprised?" asked Lucia, eyeing another piece of artichoke on his plate.

"I kept the order to two courses of entrees and appetizers after I saw Adeline's text that she couldn't make it," replied Simon.

"Bad combination of babysitter canceling and her husband traveling," said Lucia of their friend. "Thanks for ordering. What did I do to deserve you?"

"I've heard that before, usually with irritation," Simon remarked dryly.

"It's a versatile phrase that applies to *all* kinds of situations," laughed Lucia.

Simon gave a chuckle, then gestured behind her. "Here's the wine I ordered."

While the waiter poured a glass of white for each of them, Lucia leaned comfortably into the booth. Letting her eyes wander, she took in the view of the restaurant, so busy that every seat was filled.

There was a quiet murmur of laughter and conversation from the curved bar behind Simon.

They'd met during freshman year orientation at NYU, each navigating the bright, free world of being eighteen in college. Sharing a mutual love of spicy food and his hometown of Seattle, they also discovered that their fathers were both pilots. Being a native of Manhattan, Lucia had been able to watch the city open itself to Simon, who was equally tireless. After classes each Friday, he'd plot out their evening plans like a six-point strategy game, dragging her to karaoke bars in Alphabet City or taking her dancing on the Lower East Side even though she was far shyer than he was. Once, she'd even let him convince her to go all the way to Queens for a house party so he could meet up with a boy he liked. It was a hot and humid July night, with EDM blasting way too loud. That night, seeing her best friend kiss a boy beneath string lights on a crowded patio was like being thrust a bundle of thorned stems to carry. *I have no one.* So sunken in by her loneliness was she that eventually, Lucia ducked out of sight to lean against the house, whose wind-worn siding rattled each time the AC rumbled to life, so she could cry.

If Simon noticed her melancholy, he never commented on it. It wasn't until years later when they were leaving one of her mother's elegant and famed dinner parties, where wine and criticism flowed in equal measure, that Simon turned to her with clear eyes and said, "Now that I've met her, I get why you always seem somewhere else, even in a room full of people," and it made her feel less alone.

Gradually, their friendship grew out of house parties and bars.

Instead, they'd find themselves drinking beers on the stoop of her apartment, talking late into the night about their future selves in a way that only good friends can. At thirty, they'd been ecstatic to each receive a job offer at the United Nations—she in the Environmental Affairs office and Simon in the Security Council. Nearly fifteen years of friendship meant Simon had become more than a friend. He was part of her chosen family. Her real family was far more complicated.

"How's your dad?" asked Simon.

"The same, I think." Lucia's fingers grazed the stem of her wine glass. "Still flying with the same carrier, still married to you-know-who. Last we spoke was a while ago, maybe a few months? He was on his way to Dubai for an extended trip."

"Oh, well, my dad actually ran into him a few days ago," said Simon slowly. "He mentioned something about your mom."

"What about?" asked Lucia, taking a sip of wine. She thought something tugged at the corners of his eyes, but it disappeared.

"I—It's a bit of a game of telephone. I'm not really certain. But maybe call?"

"Sure," said Lucia as the food arrived. "I'll call sometime this weekend."

Partway through dinner, Lucia collapsed into laughter while listening to Simon dispense recent dating anecdotes about a man he'd met on eHarmony. He sighed in resignation.

"Honestly, I didn't even know they were still in business," teased Lucia.

"Of course they are—there are still millions of us in the five boroughs looking for handsome, rich husbands."

"Listen, if you just hold the handsome and keep the rich, there are men aplenty in Manhattan."

Simon was rolling his eyes when her phone buzzed in her bag. She showed him the screen before answering.

"Hi, Dad," answered Lucia. "Simon and I were just talking about you."

Simon had an inscrutable, focused expression. *What?* Lucia mouthed.

"Lucia. I ... " said her father. His voice, familiar and clear, cut through the noise of the restaurant. "I need to talk to you."

She sat up straight at the register of his voice. Simon's hand gripped hers across the table. "Why are you looking at me like that?" she whispered.

"Lucia?" her father's voice dragged her attention back.

"I'm here."

"Your mother. She—" A chill ran down her spine. "She passed away this morning."

Her heart stopped, air filling in the space where it should have been beating.

"Lucia?"

"What?" she breathed. "What do you mean she died?"

"Your mom ... she's been really sick. I'm so, so sorry." The somberness of her father's voice held something low and rasping, like something close to regret. "I wanted to tell you."

"I ... I don't ... " Lucia shuttered her eyes. She cupped her forehead in a daze. "She's always been so healthy. What was she sick from?"

"She was diagnosed with cardiac sarcoma about four months ago. It's a rare cancer affecting the heart. Treatment was aggressive, with discussion of surgical resection. But ... " he drifted off. "Specialists said it had progressed rapidly, too fast. We were—too late. Hospice helped her be at home in the end."

Every word from her father was an echo, like a shout into a canyon. Over and over and over, resounding in her chest. Lucia imagined a machine beeping in the corner of her parent's bedroom, monitoring Rowan's heart rate. The view of the world her mother would have seen through their framed, arched window for one final season.

" ... it was impossible to convince her to say something," her father was saying. "She didn't want anyone to see her sick. I wanted her to call. I tried several times to talk her into it, Lucia. But ... you know how she is when she's made her mind up about something."

"Are you okay?" Lucia whispered, stunned.

"There's a lot to do right now." A brief pause. "I've had more time to prepare for this."

His words were a glass house shattering between them. She took in a shuddering inhale. "Will there be a funeral?"

"I'll send you details for the memorial service on Sunday," he said, his voice thick. "I should tell you—your mother also requested to be cremated. I want to prepare you that there won't be a casket."

She was overwhelmed. Her father had been planning a funeral, and she hadn't even known. "I—should I—" Words fell short of what she was trying to say. The room had lost all of its oxygen. "I'll be there."

By the time she hung up, Simon had made his way over to her. He reached for her arm and grabbed her bag.

"Shouldn't we pay?" To her own ears, she sounded far away.

"I took care of it. Let's go."

"Simon—"

He pulled her gently to the door of the restaurant. The view appeared the same, but everything in her felt different, rearranged. The chatter of strangers, once delicate sounds in the background, now felt like a small rattle in her sternum.

Stumbling out into the summer air, a formation of birds above her head crossed towards the horizon at dusk. Shades of marigold and lilac streaked across the sky as if paint had been spilled together. Sunlight disappeared, its final dying breaths of color melting into night. It wasn't only her mother who had died, but something else in Lucia. Something long buried she'd left unattended. She wasn't sure if it could ever be recovered.

***

The memorial service was decorous and tasteful, like she'd always known her mother to be. Voices softly echoed beneath the cathedral ceiling and stained-glass windows. With the entrance of the church heavily lined with flowers, a cloying floral scent drifted toward Lucia every time someone walked in.

It all made her queasy.

"I always feel suffocated in churches." Lucia turned to her friend Adeline. "Remind me to leave instructions that only *you* will be in charge of my funeral when the time comes."

"Please," scoffed Adeline, placing a hand on her arm. "When it's our time, we will do as Victorian women did and simply drift out to sea."

At the front of the church, Lucia could see her father greeting attendees. Even from a distance, he appeared tired and older than she remembered. And next to him was an urn filled with her mother's ashes. It was a cowardly, illogical consolation for Lucia that even in death, she would not have to face her mother.

Simon strode through the church doors and made his way over to Lucia and Adeline. Following separately, two women walked in, their heels softly clacking against the tile. One woman, donning red hair and a sleek Chanel pantsuit, admired her surroundings, while the other, a curly blonde woman, adjusted her wide-brimmed hat.

"Are people aware this is a memorial service, not a luncheon?" whispered Simon conspiratorially so only Lucia and Adeline could hear.

"Of course they do," said Lucia frankly. She waved a hand to indicate around them. "There's not nearly enough wine for the occasion."

"Not with *that* attitude," Simon commented facetiously.

The two women craned their necks at the vaulted ceilings. The blonde turned to her friend and said, "I heard no one knew Rowan was sick."

"I know. So tragic." The red-haired woman inspected the cathedral. "But exquisite attention to detail, considering."

"Look, it's Daniel," spoke the blonde, indiscreetly pointing a manicured finger to the front.

"He's very handsome," replied the other. "I can introduce you if you'd like."

The blonde gave an affronted sniff in the air in response. "*I'm* the one who's known him for years." The air dropped in temperature as they made their way toward the front of the church.

"Some people have no shame." Lucia crossed her arms.

"Should we conduct a rescue for him?" asked Adeline with concern.

"I believe that falls within my daughterly obligation." Lucia blew out a breath. "Come with me? I'll need help prying him from their grasping, witchy fingers."

They walked down the narrow aisle together, and Lucia didn't recognize anyone seated. Then again, she had never really been part of her mother's world. She had expected many in attendance to be those who had supported or profited from Rowan's research. She had achieved great success as a museum curator of historical jewelry, establishing connections over three decades with committees and investors of museums in the US and beyond. The first piece Rowan had ever acquired, a gold and jade necklace, had even been on exhibit in Sweden once. Acquiring rare pieces of history that had survived despite war, politics, or geography was undeniably the one thing that brought Rowan joy. Her mother's focus had always been firmly fixed on her work. Lucia had stopped trying to compete for attention a long time ago.

"Dad," said Lucia. Standing before her father, she pressed her hands into his.

"Lucia. I'm glad you decided to be here," her father said with a solemn nod.

"She was my mother, after all," said Lucia with as much gentleness as she could muster. "Even if I didn't know she was sick."

"Simon, Adeline." Her father greeted them, adeptly navigating the minefield of conflict even in his grief. They each reached out to hug Daniel. "I'm glad to see you both."

"I read the obituary this morning," said Simon. A trace of unshed tears glazed his eyes. "It was such a wonderful dedication to her achievements."

Her father nodded at Simon's condolence. She, too, had read the obituary.

Rowan Starling passed away in her home on May 8 at the age of 62.

"I wish we were seeing each other under different circumstances," said Adeline. She gave him a hug.

"Thank you, Adeline," replied Lucia's father.

Rowan's extensive career as a curator of domestic and international exhibits led to multiple awards, including recognition from the New York Metropolitan Museum of Art and the National Museum of Art and Design in Stockholm.

"I meant to tell you sooner," said her father before turning to Lucia, all business. "There's a meeting with the lawyer tomorrow about the will. Will you attend with me?"

"Sure." Lucia swallowed, her breath seized somewhere between the past and the present. "Let me know when, and I'll be there," she said, biting the inside of her cheek.

Rowan is survived by her husband, Daniel, and their daughter Lucia.

She didn't know what else to say, what her role in all of this was supposed to be: a daughter who was both grieving and in shock? A daughter bound to the way her parents had always seen her and not as herself?

"We're being directed to sit," interjected her father. Lucia turned to see a man her age making his way to the front in a long, dark alb. As her father greeted the priest, Lucia, Simon, and Adeline moved to sit in the pew reserved for family. Simon, true to form, leaned in with an expression ready to gossip. His attention faced the man speaking with her father. She already anticipated his humor and welcomed it today, of all days.

"Do you think he's single?" he asked in a low whisper.

"We've seen this movie before," whispered Adeline with an eye roll.

Lucia gulped back a laugh, ducking her head solemnly lest someone assume she thought anything about this was funny.

***

Four hours and a funeral reception later, Lucia, Adeline, and Simon were in Greenwich, lying on one surface or another of Adeline's home. Simon sat at the breakfast table. On the sofa, Adeline reclined with her legs flipped up against the back cushion while Lucia sat cross-legged beside her. Two bottles were upright and empty on the kitchen counter while Lucia nursed a glass of wine in one hand.

Adeline's husband, Reese, was busy putting their son to bed down the hall. Toys were strewn across the living room floor, and family photos were framed on shelves. Lucia loved being in the tidy and comforting space of Adeline's house. It was like a second home. Their friendship spanned decades, their mothers having met in a Lamaze class during their second trimester. Lucia was born first, with Adeline following a few weeks later. In contrast to Lucia's olive skin and green eyes framed by dark lashes, Adeline's golden brown eyes were set against dusky caramel skin. Growing up, Lucia had always been wonderstruck by how beautiful and funny she thought her friend was. Adeline always took the short route of directness when she had something to say, and Lucia trusted her because of it. Memories of them together spanned Lucia's life, including the rebellious and monotonous. Adeline was the sister she'd never had to ask for, sharing secrets and laughs. Whole days spent lounging and people-watching in parks around the city. Adeline was the first person Lucia told when she lost her virginity. Lucia's first call after Rowan had said those seven terrible words that took Lucia's breath away: *I never wanted to be a mother.* In the years of her friendship with each of them, Simon and Adeline seemed to quietly understand that her loneliness was, like so many things, about her mother.

"Who needs a refill?" asked Simon from the breakfast table a few feet away.

"More says I," implored Lucia with a lift of her glass.

"Hear, hear," agreed Adeline, moving to sit right-side up.

"Is it in poor taste to be drunk after my mother's funeral?" Lucia wondered aloud.

"I'd argue getting at least a little bit drunk is the *only* acceptable response." Simon tipped the bottle on its end, the last drop pouring into Lucia's glass. "Another bottle, and I'll need to start charging," he drawled before returning to sit.

"Speaking of charges … " began Lucia while she examined the liquid contents of her glass.

"Hmm?" Adeline twisted toward Lucia.

"How am I supposed to bill my mother for all these years of therapy?" She hadn't meant to, but the question was punctured with imprecise derision.

"You could always send them to your dad," said Adeline with a shrug.

"That's what a daddy is for," Simon sing-songed.

"No, no, she's talking about a *father*, Simon," retorted Adeline in mock affront. "Not a *sugar* daddy,"

Lucia giggled, taking another sip of wine. "Simon, aren't you dating what's-his-face from that mega-rich tech company?"

"Yes!" Wine sloshed in Adeline's glass with as much enthusiasm as her nod. "Let's bill him for Lucia's therapy."

"Did Simon tell you how much that guy makes being VP? Like three million a year." Lucia gave a waggle of her brows. "With *bonuses.*"

"Woah." Adeline whistled. "Three million is some gold-digging territory."

"You know what they say," Simon tutted. "You are your thoughts—"

Peals of their laughter filled the room as Reese walked in, to which he merely arched a brow. He gave a kiss to Adeline before leaning down to put a hand on Lucia's shoulder. The sincerity of it sobered her, but she didn't want it to. Mostly, she felt nothing, and she wanted to keep feeling nothing. Recklessness beckoned her to drink to fill the hole in her chest. Numbness had replaced the space where her anger had been and was far more pleasant. Adeline made her way to the kitchen, leaving Lucia alone on the sofa.

Was she expected to go to work and read emails and brush her teeth like her mother hadn't just died? She recoiled from her own uncertainty and bitterness, knowing that Rowan hadn't even told her she'd been sick in the first place. Was it to punish her?

Lucia picked up her phone after hearing it vibrate. It was a notification from one of her travel apps, and her screen slowly loaded a flashing sale ad. The low purr of alcohol helped her tune out the soft, familiar voices of Adeline and Reese. Italy swam into focus, with photos of celebratory, cheery strangers posing in front of the Colosseum and over-exposed photos of cafes. Though she was beginning to feel drowsy, she tapped the screen a few times, and her phone auto-filled boxes with her name and card number. Blinking, it took a few times until, eventually, she had a small triumph of a confirmation screen. Setting her phone down, she placed her wine glass beside it.

Reese's voice was low while he spoke to Adeline in the kitchen. Through two half-lidded eyes, she witnessed a glint of something tender between them that she hadn't felt in a long time: intimacy.

She curled up on her side and closed her eyes to the slight spin of the room. A barely imperceptible shift of the cushion suggested someone sitting at her feet. The gentle, familiar hand of Simon rested on her arm, though she kept her eyes shut. Her cheek rested against the sofa fabric as sleep dragged her into its dark den. Everything was quiet now. Maybe she would be safe here, she decided, far from the grasp of where sorrow could find her.

Chapter Two

In screeching succession, both the F and A trains arrived on the subway platform.

"F train, Stillwell to Coney Island," intoned a booming voice in the station. The announcement was shrouded by voices of businessmen on phones and raucous teenagers pushing their way into empty seats. Lucia stepped onto the train with her mother. They made their way to an available row, and she wrinkled her nose at an upturned hot dog. From where Lucia and her mother sat, the denizens of New York City occupied themselves with various quirky tasks, absent of any kind of self-consciousness; one woman brushed her hair, a paper bag of groceries between her feet. Through the doors of another train car, a man came by to sell DVDs from a duffel bag.

It was her eleventh birthday, and her mother had surprised Lucia with a trip out of Manhattan. After a few stops, she began to grow more curious about their destination.

"Do you want to know where we're going?" asked Rowan.

Lucia nodded eagerly, in high spirits that her mother had planned something for them to do together.

"I'm taking us to Coney Island!" exclaimed Rowan with a wide smile on her face.

A gulf of dread yawned before Lucia, so large she could feel herself falling in.

"Aren't you excited?" Rowan's voice faltered, disappointment filling each word like water in a cup.

Coney Island was an amusement district in a nearby borough with roller coasters and rides. Lucia's fear of heights made her palms clammy just thinking of the topmost part of a ride, and she couldn't understand why her mother would choose this place, of all places, for her birthday. Lucia shrugged, her shoulders rising to meet the wavy mass of dark hair. She picked at the cuticle of her left thumb.

"Once we get there, you'll change your mind," said Rowan, patting Lucia's arm. "Roller coasters are *so* fun. I used to come here with a classmate when I was your age. Every time a roller coaster ride ended, I'd hop in line for another one."

Lucia's stomach plummeted. Keeping her eyes fixed to the window, Brooklyn passed by outside. "When is Dad coming home?" Lucia's subdued voice could barely be heard over the high-pitched wail of wheels on the tracks.

"Tomorrow. He'll call home tonight to wish you a happy birthday."

Lucia scuffed her white Keds against the rubber floor and nodded, not wanting to cause a fuss.

"I know him being gone a lot isn't easy," said Rowan with a sigh.

"But we'll take pictures and show him when he comes home."

"Will you take a picture of me with your camera?" Lucia sat up with enthusiasm. "I decided I want to take a photo of myself on every birthday until I'm eighteen years old."

"We'll see," Rowan sounded reserved. She stood as the train rattled in arrival at their stop. "Seven more years is a big commitment for someone your age."

Making their way out the double doors, her mother led the way, a light scent of lily and eucalyptus trailing behind her. Lucia stayed close to Rowan, passing a woman peeling grapefruit, the rind curling in like a wave. The citrus smell was long forgotten as the bright and fast-paced world of Coney Island greeted them. A roller coaster carried a dozen riders around on a steep loop. Their shouts and screams made Lucia's mouth dry. As she wiped her palms against the pleats of her new dress, her mother's phone began to ring.

"I need to take this. It's about a delivery for an upcoming exhibit. Why don't you take a seat over there?" Rowan pointed to a nearby bench. "Oh, don't be like that, Lucia. It won't be long."

Without another word, Rowan stepped a few feet away, one finger to her ear. "Hi, Bonnie. Yes, I've informed New Zealand that the pieces are shipping out to them tomorrow and should arrive at—"

Lucia peered up and down the Riegelmann boardwalk. The sun was at its highest point, and she squinted at it through small gaps in her fingers. Couples holding hands walked past. A young girl no older than Lucia wore a tee shirt depicting Hello Kitty doing a karate kick move at Pikachu. Lucia giggled a little at that.

Checking to see if the call was almost over, Lucia looked to where she'd last seen her mother.

Rowan wasn't there.

Hesitating, she vacillated between following the instructions to stay and leaving to find her. How long had it been? How far could she be? Maybe her mother wanted a quieter place for her phone call.

Where are you where are you where are you.

Lucia traced a path along one side of the fence, away from the noise of the theme park. She passed by a couple who seemed to be in the middle of an argument. She didn't recognize their language but felt desperate enough to ask them for help.

All of a sudden, a shadow towered behind her. Lucia spun.

"Are you lost?"

A man she didn't know stood before her, blocking the route back to the sidewalk. Despite his sunglasses, she could see beady eyes fixed on her behind dark lenses. His overlarge hands, covered in wiry blonde hair, were awkwardly shoved into his front pockets. Glancing behind him, she realized the couple arguing had left, leaving only her and this stranger. She was alone.

"I'm okay," said Lucia. She took a step away from the man, nearing closer to the fence.

He shuffled one foot forward, slowly advancing in her direction. It reminded her of the way zookeepers in nature documentaries approached wild animals before they hooked a net on their necks. He was close enough that she could smell the mint of his gum and the bitterness of his cologne.

As if pondering something, he scratched at his goatee. "Are you lost?"

Lucia stayed silent. It was hard not to notice a sizable crease in the pale green of his shirt, giving him an unsettled, disheveled appearance. Dark circles under his arms were halfway damp with sweat.

"I think I saw your mom on the other side of the street from here. I can take you if you want." His voice was coated in a veneer of honey and kindness, but there was a falsity to it that Lucia didn't trust. Something about the thinness of his lips stretched over vividly white teeth made her afraid.

"Hey!" A deep voice called out. "Everything alright over here?"

A guy in his twenties stood behind them in an orange shirt. It bore a logo on both sleeves that read, "Coney Island Lifeguard."

"Is this a friend of yours?" asked the lifeguard.

"I—" Lucia started. Her eyes darted toward him, and she stepped in a wide half-circle at a distance from the man. To her relief, he stayed where he was. She took a step away from the fence and him. Without turning, she could sense the man's attention like a phantom lingering over her shoulder.

The lifeguard guided her away from the secluded side of the park fence. After a minute or so of walking in silence, the lifeguard brought her to an empty bench close to where she'd lost sight of her mother. The seat of the hard plastic bench was warm against her legs from the afternoon sun. The lifeguard kneeled, and Lucia's hands trembled as she picked at the skin near her thumbnail.

"You didn't know him, did you?" he asked. Sunglasses were

propped at the top of his head as he waited for her to answer.

Shaking her head, Lucia swallowed so hard in an attempt not to cry that she bit the inside of her cheek. A metallic taste filled her mouth.

"Did you come here with someone? Your mom or dad?"

"My—my mom. She went to take a call," said Lucia. Waves crashed in the distance.

"Do you know how long ago that was?"

"I ... I don't know." Lucia hung her head and gave a quick shake. "I don't have a watch."

"Do you know her phone number?"

She met the eyes of the lifeguard, whose dark brown hair swept over his forehead with the breeze. "I—I only know the number at home. But my dad isn't there either. He's working."

A sigh. "I'm Austin. What's your name, kid?"

"Lucia. But I'm not a kid. I'm eleven."

He gave a smile she'd seen adults give her before when they thought she was still very young. "Nice to meet you, Lucia."

"Are you named Austin, like the city?" Curiosity had replaced panic, and she let go of the breath she'd been holding.

"Exactly," said Austin with a chuckle. "Except I'm *way* cooler than Texas." He paused. "Is it okay if I wait with you here until your mom comes back?"

She nodded, and he sat beside her. He didn't try to make her talk again while they waited. Lucia watched people pass by and thought about how thirsty she was. Then, her mother appeared, her phone still pressed against her ear like she'd never left. As she spotted Lucia, she made her way over.

"I'll be there first thing in the morning to ensure I'm there before the shipping company arrives. Yes, of course. Talk tomorrow."

Lucia took giant gulps of air, filled with relief. Noticing, her mother narrowed her eyes when Austin rose to stand. From where Lucia sat, her mother's head blocked the sun in a perfect halo. "What's going on?"

"Are you aware your daughter has been alone for close to an hour?"

"Sorry, who are you?" Rowan motioned a hand at him before narrowing her eyes at Lucia. "She knew to wait for me here."

"Someone approached her and seemed like he was trying to lead her away from the park. I only noticed because I had just gotten off my shift."

"What man?" Her mother asked in disbelief, attention swiveling to their surroundings.

"He's long gone." Austin placed his hands in his pockets. "You know this could have been a much different scenario if I hadn't seen him cornering her, right?"

Her mother gave a quick, high laugh. "You're a bit young to be lecturing me, don't you think? Everything is fine. Lucia, tell him you're fine."

"I—I thought you left—" managed Lucia, shooting a nervous glance between Austin and her mother.

"I didn't go anywhere far," her mother said defensively. "I was only a few blocks away."

Austin stared at Rowan for a long time, his expression implacable. Turning to Lucia, he gave a brief but tight smile. "Be careful, kid. Watch out and take care of yourself, okay?"

Rowan watched while he ambled away from them and toward the street. "Did something happen?" She took a seat beside Lucia.

"Not really," said Lucia, eyes aimed down at her hands that fidgeted in her lap. "A man said he knew where you were, but he was *really* creepy. He smelled, too. Then, the lifeguard found me and brought me to the bench. We waited here until you came back."

"You know better than to wander from where I told you to wait." The sharp exasperation in her mother's voice returned. "Anyway, I wanted to stretch my legs while I was on the call. I wasn't far."

"I couldn't find you."

"Listen, I know it was a long call, but I needed to settle on last-minute details with Bonnie about an important piece going out for shipment. I couldn't be there since I took off for your birthday today."

Lucia felt helpless to answer. She held herself at each elbow as she stared out toward the water.

"Let's not spoil the day," said Rowan. "Why don't we go on one of the rides or walk around for a bit?"

"Can we go there instead?" asked Lucia, pointing to the beach.

"If that's what you want." Rowan gave a brief tilt of her head. "Let's take off our shoes first."

With shoes in their hands, Lucia followed her mother. Bicycles strode past them while the waves rolled onto the shore. With her back to the sea, Lucia peered out to the rides from a distance. Sitting in a dry patch of the beach, Rowan played with the jade pendant on her necklace. Over the years, Lucia had noticed her mother's habit of spinning the pendant within its golden frame. Now, it glinted between her fingers. Rowan had told Lucia the story of how it was the first piece her mother had ever found, and it was the only one she'd kept. Lucia moved to sit next to Rowan, the sand hot beneath the fabric of her dress. The silence between them created a ball of anxiousness in Lucia's stomach. Silence usually meant something was wrong.

"Are you mad?" asked Lucia. She fumbled with her feet until they were buried and unseen in the sand.

"No," said her mother. Then, a sigh. "I am sorry. My phone call wasn't supposed to be so long. It's just one of the most important exhibits of my career. I need it to go well."

Sea foam and ocean spray filled their senses. Waves receded, pebbling the beach with small perforations. Lucia imagined all the creatures that lived beneath them that they could not see, and it brought her comfort somehow. She wrapped her hands under her knees. The sun had grown harsh in the hours since their arrival, though bursts of cool breeze enveloped them. Beside her, Lucia heard the sound of a shutter as Rowan took a picture of her. Rowan gently put the camera and its strap in Lucia's hands.

"For your birthday."

With wide eyes, Lucia held the small weight of the metal frame.

"I can have it? Really?"

"Yes. So you can do the birthday photo project you talked about," said Rowan over the roar of the water. In a rare display of affection, Rowan gently eased hair off of Lucia's forehead. Their eyes, green and oval, were mirror images of each other. Contrition was a brief shadow across her face, there and gone in a blink in the sunlight. Before Lucia could lean into the touch, Rowan withdrew, shifting her attention far away from where she felt it possible to reach her mother.

Chapter Three

The next morning, sunlight seared behind Lucia's eyelids as the world blinded her with its greeting. She awakened to Adeline's son, Theo, putting dozens of Barbie stickers on her forearm.

"He only does that to people he *really* loves," remarked Adeline, biting back a laugh. She handed Lucia two aspirin and a cup of coffee. Lucia left shortly after, with a hug and a promise to call after the meeting with her father and the attorney.

An hour later, Lucia ascended the steps of the estate attorney's office a little after 11:00. The male receptionist brought her into a large office. The room had floor-to-ceiling windows along one wall and two leather sofas facing each other. Coffee and tea sat on a silver tray in the center of an ornate, low table. Waiting for her were her father, the man she presumed to be the attorney, and Corinne, Adeline's mother. Lucia's heart lifted at the sight of a familiar face.

"Lucia." Corinne stood, reaching her hands for Lucia's.

"Adeline told me this morning you'd be here." Lucia gave a warm smile, trepidation about the meeting loosening its grip on her. Years of memories ebbed between them; she'd always felt welcomed and part of Adeline's family because of how lovingly she'd been embraced. It was the same affectionate nature of Adeline's mother that also confused Lucia. Given how different they were, Lucia never quite understood how Corinne and Rowan had remained friends.

"I only got the call from the attorney after the funeral reception. I didn't know I'd see you again so soon." Corinne pulled back to study Lucia.

Her dark hair twisted in long, neat braids over one shoulder, and Lucia was struck by how Adeline took after her. Lucia wondered if she, too, resembled Rowan in a way only others could see.

"I'm Paul, Paul Obering," interrupted the attorney with an offering of a charming smile and outstretched hand. He stood taller than Lucia, with dark hair offsetting a square jaw. "Can I offer you coffee or tea?"

Lucia worried more caffeine would make her jittery. She shook her head politely in decline. "I assume you're the estate attorney?"

"I am," said Paul, giving a wide grin so incongruous to the mood of the occasion that it threw her. He seemed a man captivated by the vanity of his own attractiveness, a frequently encountered trait that had the opposite desired effect on Lucia.

She firmly retrieved her hand as the attorney continued to smile. Lucia's father stood up to greet her. "Dad." Her voice carried a hesitation she'd wanted to conceal, but it had managed to make an appearance anyway.

His eyes crinkled slightly at the corners, while hers felt wan in return. A vague ache from last night's wine made everything feel hollow. Every movement felt robotic and stilted. She wanted to be at home, two duvets deep, with the curtains closed to the world.

Paul turned to stand at the head of the table between each sofa. "I'm sure you've wondered why I've gathered you here today," he announced. To their resounding silence, his grin faltered. "It's just a little good*will* humor."

Corinne and Lucia exchanged meaningful looks.

"Alright, maybe not that good." Paul winced sheepishly. He turned to his desk to read from an affidavit. "So, I'll begin today by reading the terms of the will set out by Rowan Starling, which was modified seven weeks ago and filed accordingly with the court. Corinne," said Paul, turning to her. "Mrs. Starling directed that two Tiffany lamps and an original Ansel Adams photograph of the 'Moon and Half Dome' be left to you."

Corinne bit her lip in an attempt at composure. Paul politely offered a tissue box, which she readily accepted.

She turned to Daniel. "Years ago, we attended an Ansel Adams exhibit together at the National Portrait Gallery in D.C. I loved this piece."

Lucia knew the story. Her mother had won it at auction, and she'd suspected her mother bought it *because* Corinne loved it, to make sure she could own a thing her friend had wanted. That is who she knew her mother to be.

"You'll find in the notarized document," continued Paul, "that $100,000 was set aside in a trust account prior to Rowan's passing. This trust and one additional item are bequeathed to Lucia Starling."

Lucia's head snapped up. She had thought her attendance was a mere formality. It hadn't occurred to her that she was still in the will. Her father noticed her shock as the attorney read the rest of the document.

"The Manhattan estate and other belongings, including all retirement, savings, and checking accounts, have been transferred to Daniel's name," finished Paul.

"What item are you talking about?" Lucia blinked slowly. "I don't understand."

Paul held up the affidavit as if it explained everything. "It is a twenty-four-karat gold pendant with imperial jade."

Lucia accepted a black rectangular box from his outstretched hand. As if in slow motion, she raised its lid to find the necklace. It was as she remembered.

The smooth gold chain lay delicately on velvet. On every third link, gold encircled a small round piece of jade. Its largest pendant, oval in shape, twirled at the end. If Lucia held it up, she knew it would pirouette half a dozen times in the light. Rowan had found it by complete accident, folded in a secret compartment within a vintage jewelry box at a flea market in Los Angeles. The necklace was beautiful and unassuming, but it was much later that her mother discovered just how precious and rare it was.

Only once had Rowan loaned it for an exhibit held in Stockholm nearly two decades ago for an exclusive three-month display. It was the longest period of time the necklace wasn't in her possession.

It was part of almost every memory Lucia had of Rowan, innocuous or indelible. It was part of her mother, and seeing it lay silently in the box was surreal. This wasn't a gift; it was her mother trying to haunt her from the dead.

"I can't accept this." She shut the lid, thrusting it to the attorney, who looked aghast. The box was heavy in her hands as she whirled to her father. His eyes seemed to witness something in her, and she loathed whatever proof he'd found that she herself could not see.

"It was the one thing she always told me belonged to you," her father managed to say.

"Bullshit," she snapped. "Did you ask her to leave me something out of your own guilt?" Lucia gestured to the box still in her hand. "I only needed *one* thing, which was for her to be someone who cared. You were there that night," she pointed in the air at his chest. She didn't care that Corinne and Paul were there. She was already hurt, already humiliated. Her father had always been soft spoken, averse to conflict. Every argument led him to agree in favor of Rowan because it was easier.

There was a sudden and emotional effusion inside Lucia. All of the unspoken words she had wanted to say to her father rushed to the surface. Her mother's death had unleashed a five-year wildfire, and she was tired of burning alone.

"I heard every word of that last conversation," Lucia bit out. "You didn't defend me when she said she never wanted to be a mother."

"Lucia," whispered Corinne, attempting to draw her attention away. "I know your relationship was very difficult. Rowan was a …

very complicated woman, but your dad is telling the truth. More than once, she told me she wanted you to have it."

"*She* should have told me herself," replied Lucia. "Did she even tell you she was sick?"

Lucia immediately regretted her words. Corinne leaned back in her seat, an injured expression on her face.

Paul cleared his throat and handed her a white envelope. "There is a letter addressed to you as well."

In her hands, Lucia immediately recognized her mother's handwriting.

Starling darling.

An enduring nickname she'd been given as a child. She traced the soft cursive of the letters. Filled with combustible intensity, rage coiled inside her, ready to spring out. Long-forgotten memories with her mother chimed from a corner of her mind: the tenor of Rowan's voice, Rowan gently cleaning pieces at her desk in the basement, Rowan's hands twirling the jade on its chain. Lucia looked down. She'd forgotten they'd always had the same hands.

"Keep it, or at least consider keeping it," her father said lightly. "She was emphatic that you have it. It's yours to do with what you want."

"I can't do this right now." She stood up to leave. "I really—I need to go."

"We still have—" Paul stopped at her expression.

Her father brought a palm into the air. "It's fine, Paul. Let's let her leave."

Lucia shoved the unopened letter and velvet box into her handbag. Without turning, she ran down the steps, the necklace bulky in the pocket of her bag. She'd take the train north, toward Central Park. The F train rattled and shook on its route towards 110th Street. She wondered what her father had seen in her during the reading. Maybe she reminded him of *her*—the brittle, caustic facets of her mother she'd tried to shed her entire life through distance and silence. Who she'd been before her mother's death and who she was now was a wound festering by the second. Was she still a daughter? Was she still breathing?

A notification from her phone sliced through her spiral. *What the hell?* It was an email with a twenty-four-hour reminder to check in for her flight.

The email confirmed a flight to Rome departing the next day. Lucia had a flash of being fairly drunk off wine the night before. There'd been some promotion for $200 flights to Europe from JFK. Vaguely, she remembered why she'd booked it—maybe it was the image of people happily eating Italian food? The version of herself that had booked the tickets wasn't totally unlike this version of herself now, trying to put separation between herself and memories of her mother. She was repelled by any notion of routine. Lucia couldn't imagine returning to her life, which had been upended since Thursday. Maybe she should leave New York, just for a little while. To feel like she could breathe again without grief pressing into her from all sides. She thought of the architecture and walking along the Tiber River, which were really the only things she knew about

Rome. What if it was enough?

Her finger hovered over the email as the doors of the train opened, indicating her stop. On the precipice of something inexplicable, Lucia felt compelled to run toward an unwritten path. Her chest rose and fell. She walked off the train to stand in the middle of the platform. Decisively, a finger hit a confirmation button for the flight as the train doors shut swiftly at her back.

Since the phone call about her mother's death, Lucia knew nothing would ever be as it was. Including her.

Chapter Four

Rome, Italy

As Oliver stepped onto the train platform, his cousin Victor clutched a hand on his shoulder.

"All this to avoid traveling on a plane," chided Victor in Swedish. "Next time, maybe we knock you out and save a day of travel."

Their appearances, marked by being the same age, were similar; each was tall, with a lean build and a hint of summer in their auburn hair. As children, they had been mistaken for brothers. Oliver's good-natured disposition was accompanied by a three-day beard, whereas Victor's intensely serious demeanor indicated that outward appearances were dissonant between them beyond his clean-shaven mien.

Pushing back his hair, Oliver soaked in the fresh air, throwing his weekend bag over his shoulder. They traversed a pathway leading away from the station. It was late morning, the sun not quite in the middle of the sky. It might've been a weekday, but Rome was a bustle of arrivals, with tourists and their suitcases flooding the walkways. Oliver despised flying and was always willing to endure long journeys by train for the charm of a new place. Though he enjoyed the familiarity of his home country, he also loved to leave it. For previous trips not easily accessible by speed rail, like Israel or Latvia, he would—on very rare occasions—grit his teeth on a plane. Although he had been to Rome before, he'd never visited in the spring. It was considerably warmer in Italy than Stockholm, which they'd left the day before. Catching the attention of an available driver, they settled into a yellow taxi. As Oliver rattled off the address of their hotel, Victor took out his phone at the sound of a notification.

"I have a meeting with my client on Friday, which means I'll soon have the book in my hands," said Victor in triumph.

"This is the science fiction book you mentioned?" asked Oliver.

"Not only that—it's a first-edition science fiction novel," replied Victor, his attention still on his phone. "The writer relocated from Barcelona about the time it went out of print fifteen years ago. It took ages for me to persuade him to sell a copy."

"And?" asked Oliver curiously. "How did you do it?"

"Money is usually a very persuasive argument," shrugged Victor as he typed out a text. "Even when people think they have too much dignity to need it."

Oliver knew acquiring rare books was a new venture for his cousin. It had been hard to miss the subtle, anxious look of Victor's mother, his aunt, when Victor had mentioned a trip to Rome. Nothing had been the same since Victor's father Anders had been murdered years before, nor when Victor had ended up in jail shortly after. They were all feeling cautious about his life after he'd been released. Mopeds steered alongside the car with their exhaust pipes whirring, slowing down and speeding up. In a roundabout, traffic sped along uneven lines of old cobblestones. The city was framed by the car window, passing speedily. Paused at a red light, Oliver noticed a crowded terrace that spilled onto the sidewalk.

Next to him, Victor tapped on his phone, uninterested in the world outside. In the years since Victor had been released from jail, Oliver hadn't picked up on any signs of troubling behavior. But Oliver, once put on high alert, found it impossible to forget.

***

"Tell me again what we're doing here?"

Oliver had to shout as they stood a few meters from the door of the nightclub. Music pulsed like a heartbeat on the streets of Rome. They'd been in the city for only a few hours, but Victor seemed anxious to socialize.

"I thought we came to Italy to be a little less Swedish and a bit more Roman," cajoled Victor. Oliver disagreed, recognizing a few Germans by their conversation and a few other foreigners. Most in line were men whose eyes roved over pairs of women laughing as they made their way inside. As the line moved a few feet forward, the techno music grew louder.

"You act like you've just been told the only way out of here is by plane," groused Victor. "We're here to have *fun*."

Oliver appreciated that despite it not being his scene, Victor was trying to get them out to see the city together in his own way. They shuffled forward with the line. Once inside, strobed lights flashed neon. Reds and blues beamed in perpetual motion across the dance floor. Crowds either danced in the center of the club or sat in shiny booths, seats so dark they disappeared into the walls. It was like being inside a color wheel on drugs, and Oliver felt entirely too sober. The booming sound outside had appeared louder than where they stood at the bar, though he could feel it in his bones.

"What can I get you?" asked the bartender, a man with light, slicked-back hair. He rapidly cleaned tall glasses with a white cloth.

"Two shots of vodka and one gin and tonic," said Victor. He turned to Oliver, who gave a nod. Victor added another finger. "Make it two gin and tonics and two shots. Thanks."

Victor waved off Oliver's motion to retrieve his wallet, handing the bartender his card. "I dragged you here, let me."

Oliver tried to be heard over the music. "Next one's on me."

Victor nodded in rhythm to the bass as he signed the receipt, shoving the thin paper into his back pocket.

"So, how did you meet the book collector you're selling to?" asked Oliver as they waited for their drinks.

"What?" asked Victor, leaning toward Oliver to hear him.

"How did you meet the book collector?" repeated Oliver a bit more loudly.

"Through connections," said Victor as he waved a hand in the air. "It's good money, and I think I'm quite good at the research aspect. Plus, it pays *really* well."

"Research aspect of what?" asked Oliver, just as the bartender pushed forward two small glasses and their drinks with ice.

"Have you come to participate in an interrogation, Oliver?" said Victor as he handed him a glass. "Or in alcohol?" They took the shots, wincing at the strength of the clear liquid. "Not quite like university anymore, eh?" grimaced Victor.

Oliver placed his glass on the bar, the counter glittering like an inky constellation. He wanted to say *that was a long time ago*, but it wasn't worth the shout. Victor set his own glass down. As Oliver leaned back, he found his heels stepping on the shoes of a woman standing behind him.

"Watch where you're standing!"

He turned, ready to apologize, but she was already turned away from the bar, her long dark hair swaying. Turning to Victor, Oliver motioned his head to suggest they move away from the bar. As soon as they stepped into the crowd, a surge of bodies pressed against the counter to order drinks. The place was packed with people undulating and drinking. Oliver searched for an empty table as they passed the shouts of a group cheering, "Saluti!" Through throngs of people, he spotted a table, and they grabbed two chairs near the dance floor.

"I need to use the toilet," shouted Victor. He briefly stood to remove his denim jacket before placing it on one of the chairs. "Be a minute."

Oliver took sips of his drink before he noticed two women nearby eyeing him up and down, mouths to ears. The taller woman sauntered over in a shimmering blue mini-dress, refracting light like a disco ball. She was pretty, with fair features and a slim nose, but Oliver wasn't in the mood to hold a conversation under the dizziness of lights and music. Her friend trailed after her through a cluster of people dancing.

"Has anyone told you before you look like a cop?" The woman in blue spoke loudly, but he could barely hear her over the bass of the music.

Oliver narrowed his eyes at the question. He inclined his gaze toward her.

"I aim to surprise," said the woman in accented English. With long fingernails, she gestured to the woman behind her. "My friend Lina and I were placing a gamble, as one might say, of the occupation men in this club might have."

With a stiff smile, he didn't answer. The women continued to stand in front of him expectantly.

"I'm Mia, by the way," she said coyly. She fiddled with her bracelet, emeralds flashing in the lights. The thumping sound of the music vibrated beneath their feet. "We're in Rome for the weekend."

He knew right away that Victor would be better company than him. The women, tall and beautiful, seemed mostly bored, which his cousin would likely accept as a challenge. The lights were giving him a headache, and he wasn't interested in making small talk. He spotted Victor returning to the table. His cousin's attention immediately went to the woman who called herself Mia.

"Am I right? About you being a cop, I mean," asked Mia. Her eyes lasered on Victor's, throwing an interested glance his way.

"What's this about?" asked Victor with a charming, curious smile. He had a type, often fixating on tall, pretty redheads.

"Mia and I were trying to guess the occupation of your friend," said Lina. "I guessed finance."

Victor gave her a brief glance before turning to Mia. "You were close, but he's not a cop," Victor's voice barely carried over the noise. He placed a hand on Mia's arm. "Do you want to sit?"

Her only answer was a flirtatious smile. Behind her, Lina whispered something, and they laughed. Lina slipped away to the bar, giving Oliver a small smile.

"This is my cousin, Oliver," said Victor, gesturing. "I'm Victor. What should I call you?"

"Mia," she answered. She gave an outstretched palm, pulling him in as his fingers closed around hers. "Now dance with me."

Victor took a last sip of his drink before placing the empty glass on the table. Together, they headed to the dance floor, Victor leading Mia by the hand. Lina gave Oliver a few coy glances from the bar. He finished the last of the gin and stood to leave. He considered grabbing his cousin's attention before heading out but decided to send a text instead. He grabbed Victor's jacket so it wouldn't be left behind. Weaving around tables spliced with florescent pink bars of light, Oliver looked over his shoulder one last time, spotting his cousin. Victor's arms curved along the waist of the redheaded woman, her palms in his back pockets, holding him tight to her. Together, they swayed in a sea of rainbows, their silhouettes pressed against each other in the heart of the ancient city.

Chapter Five

Not far from the entrance of the nightclub, a man in the shadows stood watch.

Samaran shoved his hands in the front pockets of his coat. The snap and spark of his lighter glowed against his fingers. Taking a deep drag of a cigarette calmed a restless part of him. The cigarette burned, disintegrating paper. Samaran's upper lip curled slightly as he exhaled. Illuminated by yellowed light beneath street lamps, he mulled over the job he'd been hired for, which was to locate an artifact that belonged to his client. Sources had led him to a trendy club in Rome, which irritated him. He hated noise and most people, but as a private investigator, locations were unpredictable and outside his control. This particular job, with this particular client, meant the artifact he was tracking down was, of all places, in a dark nightclub. His earlier reconnaissance had led him to the few facts he had: the item was set to be sold tonight, and the person doing the selling had been to prison before. Samaran's due diligence would need to be a bit more industrious than his usual approach.

Earlier, inside, he'd pushed through half-dressed youth while the cacophony of music played at a deafening volume. It had been almost impossible to distinguish who was who inside, but he'd found exactly who he was there for. Samaran's shoes had stuck to the floor, smelling of rum and gin. Overstimulated by flashing lights and music, it was his idea of hell. But he'd always been paid a nice lump sum to live in hell, so he tolerated it. But barely.

Samaran turned toward the echoed laughter of patrons exiting. Suddenly, he spotted them together, the last of the night's stragglers. He began to follow, thinking of how far he wanted to take this. In slow, casual steps, he kept his pace staggered to avoid being seen. They turned a corner, two forms leaning against each other in a state of intoxication. He kept his pace brisk until he was out of sight. Leaning against a brick wall, a scent of detritus smelled foul to his nostrils as he peered down the long alley. With a quiet snap of his lighter, he held his second cigarette of the night between two fingers, thinking. Glancing once more down the alley, he watched them both amble through a set of double doors to a hotel.

Too easy. His smoky exhale expanded like a cloud in the night. There was enough to report. Hitting speed dial, he had to wait for the length of only one ring.

"Samaran."

"Ma'am."

"And? What do you have?"

"I have a lead in Rome. I'll be able to verify more when I cross reference identification with the front desk."

"Did you see it? Did you find it before it could be sold?"

"Ah, at this time, I can't verify, but the source gave accurate information and—

"Was the address we discussed correct? Was it a trade-off like anticipated?"

"I believe so, ma'am. I assure you that by tomorrow, I'll have more—"

"The details don't concern me. Just recover what *belongs* to me. Find out how my possessions could be stolen in the first place. Discretion is key. And Samaran," she said in a tone too casual to not be a threat, "do not disappoint me." The phone disconnected.

Samaran pocketed his cell and crushed the filtered cigarette below his boot. He left behind a dark smudge on stone that had once been clean.

CHAPTER SIX

It was just after sunrise, and Lucia immediately regretted her decision to see the *Fontana di Trevi*. Crowds flanked every inch around the stone fountain, water trickling its murmured greeting amongst strangers. She'd awakened early to get here but could see it still hadn't been soon enough. Lucia ducked to avoid being in random pictures as she weaved in and out of people cloistered together, their phones raised to memorialize the view. The fountain was surrounded by ancient white columns. The famous *Trevi* fountain winked and beckoned in the light. Finding an empty spot to sit, she shivered against the cold stone beneath the fabric of her dress.

Lucia hadn't come to Italy in search of anything, nor did she want anything from anyone except to be invisible. Her arrival in Rome had been marked by a long taxi ride, feeling the full weight of her decision to spontaneously leave New York. Policy at work dictated she had time for bereavement leave, though she felt like doing anything except *that*. Here, she wasn't Lucia whose mother had just died; she wasn't a daughter who disappointed and confused her father; she was just a person in a country where no one knew her name. The anonymity was a marvel, a liberation. It was indescribable relief.

Absent-mindedly, she twirled the jade pendant of Rowan's necklace. Somewhere between her flight from New York to the Fiumicino airport on the outskirts of the city, Lucia had clasped it around her neck. She'd considered leaving it—and everything else—back home. Even after a few days in Italy, she still couldn't explain why she hadn't.

Feeling restless, she kept moving. The city had a lingering scent of roses and diesel fuel wherever she went. The tinny of passing mopeds built up an orchestra of sound and enthralling, too—the dichotomy of how romantic and loud it all was. Her father's piloting career took her to a lot of places in the world, but she'd never quite made it to Italy. She was glad to wander unfamiliar streets, where history and culture had prevailed for thousands of years. Rome, with its musicality of language and smell of coffee and pasta, was also contradicted by the litter pressed against curbs and blowing into alleyways. Along another narrow street, Lucia came across two gentlemen playing chess. One sported tufts of gray hair, feathering out of his fedora as he postulated with his game partner. Above her, laundry hung on clotheslines, clipped with small wooden pins, like tiny hands holding clothes out to dry.

The city required nothing of her, a tourist, and even still, it was hard to deny a lingering shadow over her thoughts. The night before, silence had felt so oppressive that in desperation not to hear her own thoughts, she'd found herself in a nightclub, of all places. It hadn't worked. Loneliness had been inescapable, trailing after her such that a soapy Italian drama on the hotel room's tv was the only way she could fall asleep. She'd given a wide berth to thoughts of her last conversation with her father. Its memory was a balloon filled with something disquieting. Afraid of what would happen if she stared too hard at it, she kept moving.

As Lucia meandered past a church, tourists took pictures on the stone steps leading to the entrance. With a glimpse inside, stillness appeared in the form of diffused light slanted through stained glass windows. Stepping into a busy plaza, she unfolded a map the hotel concierge had provided her at check-in.

Church bells marked her arrival into *Piazza Navona,* swinging their echoes in the square. As she stood before *La Fontana dei Quattro Fiumi,* her fingers traced the names of each nearby street and landmark. Although it was a Thursday afternoon, the area was filled with an assemblage of so many others.

Just then, her phone vibrated. Since landing in Rome, Adeline had messaged several times, worried about her. She assumed Corinne had described the disaster of the will reading, but Lucia didn't know what to say about it. Even to one of her closest friends. When Lucia had responded with a poorly lit photo of the Tiber to reassure her friend she was indeed alive, Adeline followed suit by only sending photos in return. Some were of Theo, or the flowers on her stoop, or a random silent disco sign plastered on a light pole in the West Village. Words continued to elude Lucia, so she sent random pieces of Italy: a pretty numbered tile above a door, a half-drank *affogato*.

Now, Adeline had sent a devastatingly clever photo of Theo holding a small, printed picture of Lucia and Adeline from high school. They were young, maybe fourteen, face full of braces and youth. A bubbling laugh escaped, maybe her first since leaving New York. She needed to send something equally worthy in return; perhaps a photo of the nuns eating gelato outside the church? Or the disappointed children whose parents politely declined to buy the cheap, colorful toys that zinged at the feet of men selling them in the square? Was it really possible to capture the vibrancy of this city and what it meant for her to be here, so far from home?

Light gilded the profile of one of the figures of the *Fiumi* as the sun began to reach its peak. Raising her head at an angle, she squinted at the ethereal sight. A few feet away were restaurants and their patrons, who sat in neat rows as if in a theater. A few feet away sat a couple indiscreetly locked in an embrace. The woman tilted her head and her male companion touched her chin, kissing her. A yearning for touch came alive in Lucia, surprising her with its ferocity, its ache.

Distracted, she missed a step and made impact with another woman. Two young children scurried to avoid tripping on her legs. Her dress fluttered in an attempt to regain footing, but it was too late. Lucia over-corrected, stumbling into an occupied table. Two men lurched away from their seats, hastily trying to bring their cups upright. Her phone clattered to the ground.

Mortified, she watched helplessly as a dark stain bloomed on white tablecloth. One of the men swore in a different language, yanking a leather-bound book from the espresso spilled.

Lifting her eyes, she staggered at his expression, coming face to face with his rage.

CHAPTER SEVEN

Oliver met Victor after breakfast, and they made their way toward *Piazza Navona*. Glancing at the book in Victor's hands, he asked, "I take it the meeting went pretty well?"

"I just left the seller's flat," said Victor, giving a dramatic salute with the leather-bound book. "More than four months' salary on this one trip."

He tapped Victor's shoulder at the edge of the sidewalk. "Do you want us to go to the hotel to drop it off?"

"It's blocks away now." Victor waved a hand dismissively. "It'll be fine. The book won't leave my sight, and I'm hungrier than I am worried about it."

In the square, the sun was beginning to shimmer above the rooftops. Most of the terraces were scattered with patrons and empty tables, and they chose one of the northeast cafes to sit. Victor moved the book from his lap to the table.

"So what will you do with it next?" Oliver leaned in his chair, chilled by the contrast of a breeze and a sliver of sun across the table.

"Sell it for twice what it was purchased for, of course," said Victor matter-of-factly.

"How'd you get into this business anyway?" asked Oliver.

"An old schoolmate, actually. He knew I was tired of working at the framer's shop," said Victor with a sigh. "That place is a dead end. Now that I have this book, I'll be delivering it personally to a collector in Berlin and leave a *lot* richer."

"Are you heading straight there tomorrow?" Two ceramic cups appeared in front of them. Across from where they sat, Oliver noticed a woman in an ivory dress with a map near the *Fiumi* fountain. Her long, dark hair shrouded her profile, but something about her captured his attention.

"Linnea, is that you?" teased Victor, referencing Oliver's older sister.

Oliver turned to him. "I know you think she interrogates you, but she means well," he replied mildly. His sister, a clinical research physician, never shied away from confrontation with Victor, which meant many family gatherings were usually spent mediating between them. Sometimes, heated arguments arose from personality differences, but Oliver knew most of the family had lost trust in Victor years ago. Linnea was slower to forgive, but he saw it differently. It was Victor who had paid the price for his decisions, and it was Victor who had lost everything because of it.

"I'm heading out tomorrow, although ... I might make a stop or two along the way," said Victor. A small smile slipped through.

Oliver raised a brow at his censored tone. "Oh? For trouble or for fun?"

"Can't it be both?" joked Victor. At Oliver's expression, he replied more seriously, "I'm going to spend the afternoon with that gorgeous redhead."

"Ah, yes—the Russian who tried to guess if I was a cop," Oliver grinned.

"She's Czech," corrected Victor, rolling his eyes. "Anyway, let's leave it alone." Defensiveness edged into his voice as the afternoon bells of a church clanged in the distance.

"Will you visit her after Berlin?" asked Oliver. He folded up the sleeves of his white button-up. The afternoon had begun to warm.

"Maybe, but she actually lives in—" Victor cut off abruptly as a woman ran directly into their cafe table, startling them.

They shoved out of their chairs as both cups went sideways. It happened too fast for Oliver to save his espresso, which narrowly missed his shirt. He attempted to turn the cups upright, motioning to a waiter for extra napkins. The scent of intense espresso mixed with the afternoon sun. The woman who'd run into their table picked up her fallen phone, and he realized she was who he'd seen standing by the fountain. When she raised her attention, the first thing he noticed was how striking she was now that he could see her face. Waves of dark hair softly framed the oval of her green eyes, illuminating the space between them.

Next to Oliver, Victor let out a slew of curses in Swedish as he tore open the hardcover book. He was furious.

"I didn't mean—" she began.

Victor's gaze rose to hers, narrowing to sharp points. "Of course," he sneered. "You're an *American*."

Her expression was etched with remorse, but she straightened her spine. "Listen, I'm so sorry—"

"That won't undo the damage you've caused!" exclaimed Victor. Seething, he flipped through stained pages before throwing the book down on his chair.

She stilled. "It was a complete and total accident."

"How does that help me?" Victor snapped. His voice pitched over a cliff, attracting spectators.

"Perhaps," responded the woman patiently, "something so important to you should be kept out of reach of us bumbling *Americans*."

"Are you saying it's my fucking faul—"

Oliver placed his arm to Victor's chest to stop him from taking another step. He grabbed Victor's attention and firmly shook his head. "I think what my cousin is trying to say is that this is a really important book. But it's clear no one did this on purpose."

"Yeah?" Victor gave a harsh laugh, saying to Oliver in Swedish, "What am I supposed to do now? Does she think I'll find this kind of first-edition book at a fucking tourist shop?" He placed the heel of his palm to his temple, appearing overwhelmed.

"If this is about money, let me pay for it." Irritation was laced in the offering as she began to reach into her bag. "How much was it?"

"Do you really think," Victor spat out, "you can just fix this with money—"

"So that's a no?" asked the woman pointedly, her wallet halfway out.

Victor snapped to Oliver, "Let's get the hell out of here." While grabbing the book to walk past her, his attention was riveted on the woman's neck. "Isn't that … " Victor frowned. "That necklace is so familiar—"

Her eyes shaped to a kind of hollow wariness, as she held the jade pendant between two fingers. Victor turned away without another word. His long strides put him meters out within seconds. Oliver threw a bill on the spoiled table. Giving her a last glance, he ran to catch up with his cousin.

"You didn't need to be so cruel, Vic."

"I'm screwed," groaned Victor. "Absolutely fucked. This trip will have been for nothing if this book is completely devalued by the stains she caused."

Oliver's long legs matched Victor's pace. A Fiat zoomed by, its exhaust pipe a whirring echo in the distance. He'd assumed they were heading to the hotel until he saw they were paused on a stretch of sidewalk leading east, in the opposite direction.

"Is there a way to fix it?" asked Oliver, glancing at the book in his cousin's hands.

"I don't know. I'll figure it out," said Victor.

"Why don't we grab a proper lunch somewhere?"

"There's no way, I've completely lost my appetite. And anyway, I have plans to meet Mia."

"Who?" asked Oliver.

"The redhead." Victor switched the book from one hand to the other, back and forth, his attention far from their conversation.

"Alright. Well … let's catch up once we're in Stockholm," suggested Oliver.

"Sure." Lines were etched between his brows as he responded distractedly. "Safe travels." At that, Oliver watched him leave. At that same moment, his phone vibrated in his pocket. Glancing at the screen, he answered on the second ring.

"Oliver can't come to the phone right now; he's on vacation enjoying being an only child. Please leave a message after the tone."

"I thought you'd become funnier with age," said his younger sister Tuva with a snort, "but it seems I was mistaken."

Oliver darted out of the way as a couple walking in front of him abruptly stopped to snap photos of a colorful building. "If you called to insult me, you can do that when I'm home this weekend."

"But if I don't help you practice humility on a daily basis, who will?"

"The other one, of course."

"Linnea and I like to switch it up."

"How lucky of me," said Oliver as he continued walking through a neighborhood near the hotel. The tinkling sounds of forks littered his walk. "What are you doing today?"

"She needs a few extra hours in the lab today, so I told her I'd spend some time with her little monsters."

"You say that as if we don't know you love Alva and Zuri more than all of us."

"Accurate. While I have you, how's your trip going?"

He gave an exhale.

"*That* is the sound of a man traveling with Victor."

"Victor is ... Victor," said Oliver.

"Still hot-tempered like when we were kids?"

"Not always. But a woman ran into our table, and coffee spilled on the book Victor had just picked up. It didn't go well."

"Yikes." Tuva gave a sigh. "The book he'd traveled to Rome to purchase?"

"That's the one." Before crossing the street, he noticed a man with black hair slicked back. Even from fifty meters away, Oliver could see the man glancing his way more than a few times. Holding the phone to appear casual, Oliver paused at a lookout point facing the Tiber, all the while keeping awareness on his periphery.

"Victor can be a bit ... intense sometimes," said Tuva.

"Only when he loses his patience."

"Which you have far too much of," she commented. "It's his mother who deserves sympathy. She's the one who had to bail him out of jail."

Oliver hesitated. "We didn't lose what he lost. And not in the way it happened. We've no idea who we would have become if it had been us."

"I know, I know. I only wish he didn't make things so difficult for himself."

Though his eyes were on the river facing north, he had to fight an urge to turn and give his suspicion away. In the distance, the man Oliver had spotted greeted a woman of similar age. Together, they began walking in the opposite direction, talking animatedly.

"Hmm?" asked Oliver, distracted. "Sorry, I missed what you just said."

"Never mind what I said. Did you catch sight of a beautiful woman?" teased Tuva.

"I thought someone was ... forget it."

"Well, if given an opportunity, you should let yourself," said Tuva. He could hear a door shutting and his sister's footsteps on a flight of stairs.

"Let myself do what?" Oliver tried to focus on the conversation.

"You should let yourself be distracted by a beautiful woman." Tuva paused. "It's been ages since you've dated anyone. I worry you might become even *more* weird."

"Being alone doesn't make me weird," laughed Oliver. "Anyway, my job isn't really conducive to dating."

"Your job also makes you paranoid."

"True."

"I'm about to hop on the train in a few minutes," said Tuva. A sound rattled in the background. "But are you having a good time at least? Other than the book disaster of the twenty-first century."

"Spring is a nice time to visit Rome," said Oliver, enjoying the calm sight of the river. "You should visit sometime. Bring your boyfriend, Alfred."

"For the tenth time," said Tuva with exaggerated exasperation, "his *name* is Alexander."

"Like I said, Albert."

"I think I'm losing you in a tunnel. Bye!" Tuva laughed before hanging up.

He pocketed his phone. Feeling his appetite grow, he searched for a restaurant on his walk so he could eat before returning to the hotel to pack. Sidewalks were bursting with flowers he couldn't name and people he'd never see again, but his thoughts were filled with the woman from earlier. It wasn't only her light eyes that drew him in. It was the way she'd stood up to Victor. There was a peculiar disappointment carved into him, realizing he'd never get to ask her name. He would have to settle for what it was: a fleeting exchange forever frozen in time.

Birds chirped overhead as he walked. The trip, despite earlier events, had been a great reprieve from the chill in Stockholm. Ivy grew along doorways, pressed against the patina of hundred-year-old buildings. His visit to Rome was a talisman, a warm memory that he hoped might linger for a while, long after he'd left.

Chapter Eight

Lucia spent the remainder of the afternoon trying to shake off the encounter by walking through Rome.

Her fingers grasped the pendant, absentmindedly twirling it within its oval frame. Even in the sunlight, it was cool to the touch. Traveling to Rome had been an attempt to leave everything behind, but she was having difficulty staying true to the sentiment. She couldn't seem to outrun Rowan's memory, no matter which streets she turned down. Every cafe seemed seated with women whose dark wavy hair reminded her of Rowan. Was she walking through the same places her mother had? Was history repeating itself while she meandered through the city, thinking, doing, and feeling the same things her mother once did?

As Lucia made her way back to the hotel, she reveled in the golden light of the city. Blush hues contrasted against the faded paint of building facades and clay rooftops. Pigeons that'd made homes out of gutters and chimneys squawked above her. As she walked through the entrance of the hotel, the concierge—a small woman with an oval face sharpened by an asymmetrical hairstyle—nodded at Lucia with a smile. It was the same woman who'd checked her in the day she'd arrived. She returned the greeting with a small wave.

Making her way toward the elevator, Lucia was relieved to have the entire space to herself. The doors groaned shut and she closed her eyes, trying not to imagine how old the cable wires might be. Lucia leaned against the elevator's wood panels as it made its slow ascent to the fourth floor.

At the ding of the doors opening, she stepped out. Struggling to get the key card, her hands gingerly released the fabric handles attached to her shopping bags. When the door handle beeped, she stepped into the quiet of her room. Opening the doors to the small terrace, sounds from four floors below drifted in. This time tomorrow, she would be on a short flight to Milan, in hope that a different place would distract from memories and home and herself.

She thought about where to eat dinner as she busied herself by removing her necklace. Her fingers squeezed the clasp below her hairline. Undressing, she tossed her passport and clothes on the bed and delicately placed the necklace at the collar of a lavender dress she'd wear for the evening.

In the shower, she let herself be enveloped in hot steam. Water began to soak in the long threads of her hair. Was it ironic or tragic to come to a romantic place like Italy alone? Thinking of the man she'd seen earlier, thinking of his intensely curious gaze. The smoldering of attraction had been a string taut between them. With a sigh, she put it out of her mind. It didn't matter what he'd made her feel; she'd never see him again. She certainly didn't want to run into that *other* guy, his brother maybe, ever again.

Click

Lucia stopped midway, soap at her wrists. Her ear was turned toward the door, which was ajar to the bedroom. A distant laugh reminded her she'd left the terrace doors open. Sliding her hair to one side, water washed down her shoulder blades.

At the second *click*, she startled at the undeniable sound of the room door. Cautiously, she turned the shower handle off. Her hands gripped a white towel she used to quickly cover herself. The sink counter held nothing of use for a weapon. Slowly, she pushed the bathroom door outward until it was parallel to the wall of the room.

Nothing.

Craning her neck from side to side, everything seemed as it was before her shower. The room was empty. Relieved, her shoulders lowered, releasing a tightened grip on the towel. Her fists had been pressed against her collarbone, absent of her necklace.

She spun, her spine gripped in shock. One thought shattered like glass into a million pieces at her feet: her mother's necklace was gone.

Chapter Nine

Lucia stood motionless, her heart skipping like stones across a silent pond. She blinked rapidly at the space where her belongings had been. Missing were not only her mother's necklace but also her dress and passport. The sharp curve of her fingernails dug into her palm. In dismay, she frantically confirmed against all doubts that she was indeed still alone.

The furniture sat quietly. Nothing moved.

Less than thirty seconds had passed since she'd heard the sound of the door closing. Maybe—maybe there was still time.

She threw open the door and hurtled into the hall. Whipping her head to each side, one end was empty. At the other, a posh-looking woman wearing sunglasses and a headscarf pulled out her keycard several doors down.

Lucia abruptly ran the length of the hall. At the sight of Lucia in only a towel, the startled woman retreated in alarm, pressing her purse close against her. She kept one hand on the doorknob to her door.

"I'm not trying to take anything from you. Did you see someone leave this room just now?" asked Lucia, her voice hoarse. "My room was robbed." Adrenaline blinded Lucia. She'd been only a few feet away in the room when the necklace had been stolen.

"Ah, non," said the woman, her forehead wrinkling in confusion. "Je ne parle pas—"

Lucia rapidly switched to French, a language she'd studied and become fluent in while working with the French ambassador to the UN. She rushed through questions: Did the woman see anyone leave her room? Which direction? She held tight to her towel with one hand, while the other pointed to her exposed collarbone to explain the necklace.

"Non, désolée." The French woman spoke softly. She pointed in the opposite direction with a long, manicured finger.

An EXIT sign glowed at the end. Well past the elevator, the stairs would lead out to the street, avoiding the front desk entirely—

Lucia immediately understood. With a shout of thanks, she sprinted without another glance. The pale blue walls of the hallway passed in a blur.

Below the EXIT sign, a large metal door was visibly unlatched. When she pushed at its center, what lay beyond was nothing but an empty fire escape. Down four flights, the street was empty. She pressed it open further with a palm. Craning her neck upwards, she could see it led up to the roof.

Tense, she stepped back into the hall, the door closing slowly behind her. The outside air was light against her skin, like a feather. Lucia inhaled, gripping one hand against her towel as the other made a fist at her side. She seethed at her helplessness.

How did this happen? How was she going to get home without her passport?

A sliver of wind blew in as the door closed its final inch behind her. A few leaves and small papers had drifted in as she took a few steps in the direction of her room. She stopped. Hinging on her heel, she turned. Kneeling, she retrieved two small pieces of paper, each folded inside of each other. A receipt and a train ticket. She was astounded to see the familiar logo. It belonged to a nightclub she'd been to the other night, when she'd grown weary of being alone with her thoughts in her hotel room.

Scanning each piece of paper, she scanned it for answers. On its face was a last name, the last several digits of a card number, and an amount of twenty-seven euros listed on the bottom. Turning it over to its blank side she flipped it over. The train ticket matched the name on the receipt. Four digits of a card number and a last name with a first initial. *It couldn't be him, could it?*

Her mind turned on its wheels, thoughts rapidly firing. In her room, she firmly shut the room door. She was relieved to at least have her phone, which she'd brought with her into the bathroom. Steam had filled the room in her absence. Had it only been minutes since she'd run out?

Outrage was a noise buzzing over the sound of her thoughts while she tried to collect herself. Certain international laws meant it would be possible for her to get assistance with her stolen passport at a US embassy. Exhaling, Lucia knew she needed to immediately file a report with the police about Rowan's necklace and her missing passport. Reporting to the police wouldn't guarantee they'd locate the necklace, but her stomach lurched at the thought of never trying. She would do it, but she'd have to hurry.

Throwing a clean dress over her head, she slipped on ballet flats. Springing to the elevator, her fingers punched the down arrow. The slow hum of the elevator answered, a golden light above the doors indicating it to be on the first floor. She wanted forward momentum. Every second it took for her to get to the front desk equaled more distance between herself and the necklace. After running down four flights of stairs, she approached a hotel staff member. Tears stung as sharply as her palms landing on the countertop of the front desk.

"I need to report a crime *right now.*"

***

When a call came through the radio in his car, *Polizia Municipale* Marco Costa had his eyes on two brunettes crossing a street. Trying to avoid gaps in the cobblestone, the women continued their walk in slim black heels. Speaking with dispatch, Costa received notification of a robbery at a nearby hotel. An American woman needed to file a report, and the owner requested that it be done at the hotel. He swore under his breath, aggrieved to leave the current view of his posting. More than once, he'd filed a report for theft, only to later learn the person filing it had enough money beyond what was stolen. Experience so far had taught him most people who'd traveled with items of significant value almost always received double its value from insurance after filing a claim, especially with a police report on file. Cloaked in a strongly held belief as a martyr, he imagined himself as the first line of defense against greed.

Costa pressed a button on his radio, guessing this case was already a waste of his time. The two women passed his car, and he sighed, turning the ignition as he began his drive toward the hotel.

Despite five years as an officer, his chronic dissatisfaction only increased each time his family compared him to his younger brother, a financial investor at a bank. His job was the one aspect of his life where he had real authority. As a native Roman, his constant exposure to tourists had made him grow resentful. He'd been forced to bite his tongue each time a wealthy foreigner treated an officer in his department like they were a tour guide. Anytime he was asked, he pretended not to speak any English, which suited him just fine. Costa begrudged the way tourists trashed and disrespected every crowded sidewalk, trampling his streets, his city.

As he turned the corner to the hotel, he slowed to park. His first thought walking inside was that he'd spotted the woman right away. A slim brunette sat in the lobby, her arms crossed. Even sitting, she appeared taller than average. Her long, dark waves softened the planes of her high cheekbones. The anxious, pinched expression she wore might have given her away if he'd been paying closer attention. Instead, he honed in on her designer handbag and self-assured posture. He sighed, growing tired of helping people whose lives weren't affected by the outcome of a police report, who might go back to wherever home was and move on while he was left behind to labor with an investigation.

***

When the *polizia* arrived, Lucia was lost in thought, the fabric of the sofa scratching against her legs. Staff had brought her a coffee, though it sat untouched on the side table, growing cold. Her eyes followed the hotel owner, an older Italian man with a thin gray combover, as his hunched gaze darted to the hotel entrance. A dark-haired man in uniform walked in, his eyes narrowing in a way she immediately disliked. It made her straighten her spine despite the emotions pulling at her like a puppet on a string. As the owner rushed to greet the officer, he extended his arm in Lucia's direction. She stood for the brief formality of introductions, giving a curt nod. She studied Costa's militant haircut and unzipped navy jacket as he took a seat diagonal to Lucia and requested coffee from staff. His gaze wandered the length of the lobby.

"Officer Costa?"

"Si," nodded the officer.

"Would you mind if we start the report?" Lucia's leg twitched as his gaze rose up toward the crown molding.

"Of course," said Costa. "The coffee should be here momentarily."

"I haven't touched mine," Lucia pushed her coffee toward him. "Could we begin?"

Despite the dismissive glaze in his eyes, she tried to keep faith in the process. She was committed to it; he was already here. His proficiency in English made her grateful she could file the report at the hotel rather than at a station. A different front desk clerk handed over a coffee cup to the officer. She watched Costa's eyes, small and dark, observe the woman leave.

When he realized Lucia was watching him, he took a quick sip. He took his time sliding his coffee beside hers and removed a small notepad and pen from inside his vest pocket. Her jaw clenched, biting down on her growing impatience. As a New Yorker, she held law enforcement in high regard, but incompetence reigned in her country, too.

"Please tell me your full name."

"Lucia Starling," said Lucia with deliberateness. "S-t-a-r-l-i-n-g."

He wrote slowly. "Do you have your passport?"

Lucia shook her head. "Three items were stolen. One of them was my passport."

"You'll need to contact your embassy before traveling home," said Costa as he took notes. "I've been told you lost a necklace. Where did you last see it?"

"It's not lost," she bit out. She wanted to throttle him. "It was stolen from my hotel room. Room 424."

Costa took a sip of her coffee, then realized his mistake as he returned her cup to its matching plate. She barely tried to hide her incredulity. The fate of finding her mother's necklace rested in the hands of this ... buffoon? Someone whose attention to detail seemed displaced by anything not attached to a pair of legs?

"You're certain you didn't drop it somewhere before you returned to the hotel?" His pen was poised in the air like an afterthought.

"You're asking me if I—if I think it fell off my neck and didn't notice?" Lucia's voice was laced with agitation.

Costa's blank expression was wrapped in a lazy gauze, confirming what Lucia now knew: involving the local police was a wretched, foolish decision. "Not only am I certain I was robbed, but I don't appreciate the implication that I'm committing insurance fraud." Her fury was a bolt of lightning. "It happened here. It happened in my room."

"Ms. Starling," Costa started, "there is no need to become upset—"

"Upset?" Her heels pressed into the floor as she leaned toward the officer. "You think I'm *only* upset at someone stealing my mother's necklace? Shouldn't the hotel be concerned that someone broke into a guest's room?"

"Yes, of course," hesitated Costa, as if suddenly aware of himself.

"Is there no way to check the camera footage in the hallway?"

At that, Costa spoke in Italian to the hotel owner, who'd stood a respectful distance away. Listening to the exchange, Lucia turned at the waist. The owner responded, pointing to each corner of the open lobby and behind the front desk. Watching their body language was like absorbing truth by osmosis. Agonizing hope ballooned in her in the silence, wishing to be contradicted.

"There are no cameras on my floor," guessed Lucia haltingly.

"Ah, unfortunately, Ms. Starling, there are only cameras here in the lobby. There," said Costa with an index finger pointing to the concierge desk, "and at the front entrance."

"What about the back? The stairwell?" asked Lucia. She'd chosen the hotel for its quaint, classic Roman charm, and its allure would be to her detriment.

Costa rested his palm on his thigh, speaking to the manager again.

"Only the front. We could review the lobby cameras in case whoever broke into your room came in through the entrance. It could take at least a few weeks to process the footage with our department," said Costa. "The camera is very old."

The owner shifted, leaning toward Lucia with sympathy in his eyes that did nothing to soothe her mounting frustration. "*Mi dispiace*," his hands were folded in front of him as if in prayer. He seemed so small in his suit, the cuffs an inch too long at his wrists. "*Mi dispiace.*"

"Miss, if it is a matter of money, there is always insurance—" Costa stopped speaking at Lucia's expression, shrinking. It was the first time he seemed to really respond to her.

"You think—you think this is about money for me?" seethed Lucia. Abruptly, she pulled the folded receipt from her purse, practically shoving it into Costa's hands. "This is a receipt and train ticket. The names on both match." Lucia leaned forward, elbows at her knees. "I found it near the exit door where I believe the person ran out. I think this belongs to whoever took the necklace."

He turned it over in his hands a few times. "This is a hotel, Mrs. Starling—"

"It's miss, I'm not married."

"This could have been left by another guest." He returned it to her, almost patiently, as if she were a child.

She wanted to scream. To tear the receipts in his face as if it would prove a point. Instead, she sank into the chair. He wouldn't hear her no matter what she said.

Costa finished writing something on his notepad and handed her his pen. "I will file my report for your incident this evening so you have documentation for insurance. You can send me a photo of the necklace. I will also interview members of the staff for official statements. Now, *per favore*, write your contact number so I can reach you when necessary."

Lucia began to protest but pressed her lips into a thin line. The hope had been that resources at the disposal of local law enforcement could lead to the perpetrator. She didn't have language skills, connections, nor access to their internal systems. She knew the exact person who might be able to get answers to her questions. In the task of obedience that she did not feel, she wrote her number down.

CHAPTER TEN

Lucia stepped into her hotel room, alone again. She'd lost so much time filing with the police. The report, if Costa's lack of concern was any indication, might simply be forgotten in a shuffle of paperwork and indifference.

Mounting panic seized her.

She hadn't asked for Rowan's necklace, had barely thought of it over the years. Much like her, she had wished for something different in this one life. Lucia had spent years wishing for a different mother, but Rowan was the only one she'd ever have. The fantasy had been in the hope that her mother might regret what she'd said five years ago. It was a hope Lucia had clung to, wishing for a future that could be different from what the past had been. But now, reality was a tightrope a thousand feet up. She'd never get her mother back. What would it mean if the necklace was gone forever, too?

Pulling the train ticket and receipt from her pocket, her hands gripped them tightly. They had nothing new to reveal. Just the same last name, the same last four digits of a card number. She reached for her phone. Simon picked up on the third ring.

"Luce!"

Without a preamble, she asked, "Hypothetically, would it be possible to find someone in the UN's database?"

"Oh, well, now that we have that out of the way," laughed Simon. "What time is it there?"

The clock on the bedside table. "6:32. I know it must be late—"

"Lucia Starling, it's the middle of the day."

She calculated backwards. "God, I hate math." With an exhale, she pressed her fingers to her brow bone. Music and conversation could be heard, loud and distracting. "Listen—"

"I'll find a way to love you despite it," quipped Simon.

"Simon, I really need you." Her words tumbled out, desperate to find a home.

"What is it?" his voice rising. "What's wrong?"

"My hotel room was robbed and—"

"It was WHAT?"

"I'm okay, I'm safe, but—"

"You called the police, right?"

"First thing I did. Listen to me, Simon—I need your help finding someone."

"I'll be home in ten minutes." Lucia heard him say something indistinguishable to someone nearby. "I'll call you right back."

"Alright," said Lucia, her voice barely above a whisper.

Placing the phone on the bed face up, uncertainty made her hesitate. Was she really about to ask Simon to glean confidential information? Lucia paced while her nails dug into the skin of her palm. She resisted an urge to pick at her cuticles. Sunset was still hours away, but the sky was beginning to streak with shades of dark blue in the distance. She felt numb. When Simon's name came up on her phone, she answered immediately.

"Are you okay?"

Faced with the obligation to take her emotional temperature, she didn't know where to start. "I'm not hurt," said Lucia finally. "But the person who broke into my hotel room stole my mother's necklace. There's no camera footage on this floor to go by, no evidence of the robbery except my word and my missing passport. But I think I know who did it."

"What the actual hell?"

"It's part of a longer story, but my room was burglarized after a confrontation with these two guys. One of them, maybe Dutch or Norwegian, maybe, specifically commented on the necklace. Then, I found a train ticket and a receipt from a bar in Rome, time-stamped for the same night I was there. I think they belong to him, and I think …"

"You think he followed you to your hotel," Simon finished for her. "Holy hell, I can't believe this happened to you."

"It's too much of a coincidence." Lucia nodded even though Simon couldn't see. "Maybe he followed me somehow, I'm not sure. But I found the receipts down the hall from my room *right* after I was robbed. Like they'd fallen out of someone's pocket. If I was followed, it would have been him. I'd bet money on it."

"You said you already contacted the police?" asked Simon. Lucia could hear a door opening and closing, a laptop being set on a surface.

"It was an infuriating dead end," said Lucia. "You're my last resort."

"Well, technically, Lorenzo is your last resort. The UN doesn't have access to the Interpol system, but I'm pulling in a huge favor."

"Wait—Lorenzo?" asked Lucia, surprised. "The guy from Buenos Aires you called your two-night stand?"

"Yep, that's him. The one that got away," laughed Simon. His warmth and familiarity reached its arms through the phone, offering Lucia comfort. "He's an intelligence officer."

"How the hell an intelligence officer in Argentina owes you a favor—well, maybe I'd rather not know."

"I wouldn't ask too many details if I were you," said Simon dryly.

The tension and adrenaline of the past few hours had made it difficult to remain rational. The brief respite in conversation with Simon gave Lucia pause. "Is this going to get you … fired somehow?"

"Well, I haven't even given Lorenzo any information to go on yet."

"Yes, but once you do, is searching for someone in the Interpol system going to come back to haunt us both?"

"Depends on what we find, honestly. There's something called a red notice that flags a person or issues a warrant, but only law enforcement can do that. I have limited access to information, but Lorenzo says he'll help."

Her eyes drifted to the terrace doors, laughter from below finding its way into her room.

"Okay, he's ready—what information can you give me?"

Despite her earlier bravado, she hesitated.

"Luce?"

"I'm here."

"We always said we'd do anything for each other, right?"

"Yes."

"Let me help. This is under the umbrella of anything."

She rattled off all the information on the receipt, leaning her forehead into her palm with a tremble. Lucia knew data would only be generated in the system if the person who'd stolen the necklace had a criminal record, but she was following her instinct. Simon relayed everything she had to Lorenzo.

"He got a hit and was able to pull up the owner of the card. Hmm ... the person definitely isn't Italian. He's sending me a screenshot." A second later, Simon whistled. "They've got quite the record. Theft *and* robbery."

Through her daze, she felt vindicated in not ignoring her instincts. "I know this is another ask ... but I need his address."

"The address linked to this guy? The one with the criminal record?"

"Yes."

"Why?" asked Simon.

"Because if I have the address, I can point authorities in the right direction. If there are multiple priors on this guy, it'll mean the difference between finding the necklace before it's sold and never seeing it again." She closed her eyes to the emptiness of the room. "It's the last, real thing I have of her."

"Lorenzo will do it," Simon hesitated. "But for fucks sake, do *not* confront this guy."

"Absolutely not," said Lucia seriously.

Soft tapping sounds from the keyboard could be heard while Simon typed. Her heartbeat battered against her ribs. Lucia sat at the edge of her hotel bed, feeling lightheaded as he relayed the name and address. She read the name and country she'd written on hotel stationery.

"I will call you once I've contacted the police again," said Lucia. "Does Interpol have access to financial transactions? Could Lorenzo let me know if any activity changes on the card?"

"Would you also like satellite coordinates or just hour-by-hour updates?" asked Simon wryly.

"Is that an option?" Lucia half-joked.

"Be safe and call me after you've talked to the police again. That's not negotiable, okay?"

She let out a sigh and a mumble of affirmation.

"Good." Simon's voice was firm before he hung up.

For a long time after the call, she sat on the bed, pressing all her toes into the thin hotel rug until they went white with the loss of circulation. Migrating to her laptop, she referenced a saved email with her passport number and bought a train ticket for a 9:20 evening departure.

Simon had asked her not to confront anyone, and she'd told the truth when she'd said she wouldn't. What she *wouldn't* tell him is that personally confronting the guy wasn't necessary if she rallied someone else, like, say, local police. She'd tell Simon the truth when she returned to New York, but she hoped he'd forgive her for what she was about to do.

For an hour, Lucia researched how and where to make an appointment at an American embassy in the EU. Knots formed in her stomach, knowing she would be traveling to a different country without her passport, but she was determined not to lose even more time by staying in Rome. Even if it would take over thirty hours of travel, she was resolved to keep going. Her train had brief scheduled stops along the way in France, the Netherlands, and Denmark. None of which were her final destination. As it turned out, she'd been wrong—the accent wasn't Norwegian or Dutch.

That motherfucker was Swedish.

***

At a quarter past nine o'clock, Lucia stood on a train platform. Readying herself for the long journey ahead, squeals echoed on the platform from metal wheels slowing on the track.

Passengers lined up in scattered rows, pulling luggage in various conditions behind them. Glancing at the ticket in her left hand, she shifted her luggage to the other. She'd already checked a hundred times to memorize the cabin number she'd reserved.

A dozen feet away, a man, tall with auburn hair and relaxed posture, paused in front of the slowing train. A weekend bag was slung over his shoulder. Lucia tugged at the ivory sweater keeping her warm. The doors *wooshed* open. With determination, she stepped off the platform and into the unknown.

CHAPTER ELEVEN

In the early light of the next day, Lucia watched the sun rise over Brussels. Her hands curved against a warm cappuccino as sage green hills fled sight. As more distance was put between her and Rome, she'd harbored a vicious disposition.

She'd hoped going to Stockholm would make her feel better, but with nothing to do but wait, her cuticles fell victim to her fixation. In total, the trip would be thirty-three hours long. While her private cabin was quite small, it was also quaint, designed with style and practicality by utilizing every possible inch. In a more eased state of mind, she would have appreciated the decor of dark wood paneling contrasted against silk curtains. Instead, her fatigue finally began to win out. All night, she had tossed and turned until, eventually, she'd thrown off the sheets and listened to other restless passengers walk through the hall at sunrise. Periodically, her hands kept touching where the necklace used to be.

Victor Hedlund.

He was, she'd learned, a Swedish book buyer formerly arrested for robbery at twenty two. Between his manners and the crimes he'd committed, he was guilty of a lot of things. His first conviction—petty theft—at seventeen led to a later arrest for a misdemeanor and possession of a stolen vehicle at the university where he'd been enrolled. Reports included a statement by an accomplice who mentioned plans to break into a house for an heirloom. His second sentence was longer, and he'd been released from jail about five years ago. With the help of the internet, she translated police reports Lorenzo had sent her directly.

On the face of it, Victor currently lived a very normal, private life. At least from what she could see after digging through his social media. Seeing his arrogance in every photo, anger curled in her gut. Was he one of those men who always used charm and manipulation to take things that didn't belong to him? Did he see her at the nightclub first, then follow her? Thinking about that afternoon in *Piazza Navona* ... was none of it a coincidence?

She'd scheduled an appointment at the Swedish embassy, and then she would go to the police. That would give her time to update Simon and deal with any consequences of having withheld the truth from him. Reporting Victor in his home country might increase the probability of local law enforcement arresting him, but worry had begun to grow. There was also the excruciating possibility the necklace had already been sold. Unease bloomed. Sweden was less than twenty-two hours away, but it might as well have been weeks considering the amount of unknown variables. Hope wasn't much of a safeguard, but she'd made it this far, and at one point, that hadn't seemed possible either.

A buzz in her bag got her attention. It was her father.

> Adeline mentioned you left for Italy. When do you return?

Thinking of their last conversation in New York made her stomach twist. A second message came through.

> I hope we can talk when you're home.

Gently returning her phone to the interior pocket of her bag, her head turned toward her cabin window. Her eyes pricked with disappointment. Longing was as familiar to her as breathing, but something less easy to name had formed since the news of her mother's death. Outside, the scenery changed as the train continued onward. Lucia fell asleep that way, hypnotized by the pastures of wide, green fields, lush from rain the night before.

***

New York City, Fourteen years earlier

In a cab ride uptown, the driver adjusted the volume as Bowie sang about Lady Stardust. The low voice built to a crescendo, matching the rhythm of a summer rainstorm. Lucia traced the rain droplets on the window. For her eighteenth birthday, she was meeting her mother for an afternoon at the Metropolitan Museum of Modern Art. As the driver eased over to the corner of 5th and 83rd, water sloshed along the cement steps. Stepping out, Lucia briefly opened her umbrella as she made her way to the entrance. Wind whipped the museum flags above. It was a familiar scene, cars honking and pedestrians not waiting for the crosswalk lights. Vendors selling art and food took shelter beneath canopies. Warm bread from a nearby hot dog stand drifted past as she climbed the steps of the museum. Lucia shook out her umbrella before heading inside. Below the expansive ceiling, she imagined herself as something small, as ants might feel beneath hundred-year-old trees.

Despite growing up in New York, the Met never got old. Crowds milled about in quiet murmur as they read from brochures. A reverence within the museum walls sent a familiar thrill down Lucia's spine. As a gift, her parents had paid for a year-long membership. It was a bit redundant, since her mother knew the director personally and could go anytime she wanted. Not seeing her mother anywhere, Lucia checked her phone. No messages. Deciding to head to an exhibit while she waited, Lucia flashed her membership card to an attendant before making her way up a steep set of stairs. She kept her hand on the smooth railing as she ascended. Damp markings from the rain slashed against the pleats of Lucia's dress. Her shoes bounced gracefully against the buffed steps. On the landing was a kind of intersection: two halls leading in opposite directions. Assessing her mood, she turned right for the *Temples of Dendur*. In a room filled entirely with light, slanted floor-to-ceiling windows projected a soft gray filter into the space. Each temple stood on a raised platform; their sturdy design reflected along neat edges of water, which surrounded most of the exhibit.

Despite, or maybe because of, the rain, the room was filled with onlookers, tourists from far and wide. Lucia hardly paid attention. Her last visit here had been several months before, when her mother had donated a seventeenth-century artifact and celebrated the exhibit opening. Lucia found herself standing before the two statues closest to the water. With a slender finger, she traced the words on the plaque.

"Amenhotep III," Lucia read softly to herself. She moved out of the way as a family walked by, snapping pictures of the statues. Her own camera hung over her shoulder. The rain had nearly been a deterrent today, but true to her vow, she planned to take a photo of herself as she'd done every birthday since her eleventh.

"The ninth pharaoh ruled after his father, Thutmose IV, died," said a woman behind Lucia. "I wonder how old Amenhotep III was when he ruled?"

"Mom, it says he was twelve—my age!" exclaimed a young boy. Lucia took a step out of the way. His mother pointed at the vignettes etched into the temple. They shared the same complexion and hair color.

"How old was he when he died?" The kid gazed up expectantly from the plaque.

"You're making your mother do a whole lot of math this morning," she commented with a soft chuckle.

"Good thing it's my birthday," grinned the boy.

Lucia felt a buzzing in her jacket pocket. Retrieving it, she moved out of the way for others who began to crowd in.

"Hi, Mother."

"Lucia." Rowan's voice sounded distracted, which always put Lucia on the defensive. "Are you already at the museum?"

"I am. Are you on your way?" she asked. Lucia hated the eagerness in her voice, even after all the years of trying to train herself out of it.

"I got a last-minute call from a client who is only in town until tonight. They need to meet about the exhibit next month in Seattle. We're having issues with their shipping procedures."

Lucia watched the same kid and his mother point to the temple.

"Lucia?"

"Yes, I understand."

"Listen," said her mother with apprehension. "It's only one day. Your dad and I can take you to dinner tomorrow."

"I'm not upset."

"If you're sure." Her mother paused. "I have another call, but we'll see you tomorrow. Okay? And—happy birthday."

"Talk to you tomorrow," said Lucia, hanging up first. Her black flats *clacked* with each movement across the tiled floor.

Across from her, columns leading into the temple formed the shape of papyrus stalks. The mother and her son walked past Lucia, arms hooked as they giggled and held on to each other. Lucia refused to be a New York City cliché by crying in public. She was well beyond that. It shouldn't surprise her, after all. She'd ached for closeness with her mother long enough that Lucia couldn't recall who she was without it.

***

"*Per favore*, your tickets."

Disoriented, her eyes opened from a deep sleep. The voice was paired with a small, second knock against her cabin door, which she stumbled to. She was still reeling from vivid, mercurial dreams. Pulling the train ticket from her bag, she handed it to the ticket inspector. Lucia stifled a yawn as he punched a corner of the cardstock. At his curious expression, she fidgeted, wondering if he would ask for her passport. Was this it? Was this the end of her search for the necklace before it had ever really begun?

"The cafe is two cars away," remarked the inspector with a polite smile. Pointing briefly to his left, he carried on with his ticket script as he knocked on the door of the next cabin. Returning to sit at the edge of the bed, she began to come out of her fog of inattention. Her phone showed it was now early afternoon. Daylight had turned the scene out her window from a rainy morning to a sunny, clear day.

She'd forgotten the sun would stay up much later as she continued north. Splashing water on her face in the tiny, half-moon sink, she began to feel more alert. Using one of the plush hand towels, she gently patted her cheeks. The contents of her cappuccino cup had turned cold hours ago. Restless and hungry, she was compelled to get out of her cabin in search of something more appetizing.

Walking in the direction indicated by the inspector, Lucia hoped the cafe and restaurant were in the same car. The train company's website boasted dark velvet booths, a window framing a view of the Swiss Alps. With other passengers shifting in the aisles past her, it took her a few minutes to get through two more cars before reaching the dining cabin. At the cafe counter, Lucia tried to make eye contact with an attendant at the opposite end who was pouring espresso into a disposable mug. As she made another attempt to grab the attendant's attention, she sensed someone staring. A man, tall with light sandy-brown hair and blue eyes, was studying her. She recognized him immediately.

"*You*?"

As if he had materialized from her memories, the man she'd met in Rome stood beside her.

CHAPTER TWELVE

Her eyes were as crystal clear as he remembered them. Green and sharp, like winter frost on aged vines. An astonished expression spread across her face.

"We saw each other yesterday in Rome, yes?" asked Oliver. He placed a one euro coin on the counter when the attendant handed him his espresso. The woman was gaping at him, a slow storm of irritation rumbling. He offered an upturned smile and a lift of his disposable cup. "Don't worry, this one has a lid."

"I am absolutely not amused," said the woman with a glare. "What the *hell* are you doing here?"

"Grazie, Mr. Ström," said the attendant when he lifted the euro off the counter. He gestured politely to an empty booth. "Would you like to dine with us this evening?"

She seemed to wrestle between uncertainty and fury.

"We'll need a minute, I think," responded Oliver. The attendant nodded and began to organize wine bottles in a crate a few feet away.

"I can speak for myself," she snapped. "Mr. *Ström.*"

"Please, it's Oliver," he said with a nod. "Mr. Ström is my father."

"Ok, Oliver. Between stalking and the theft of my necklace, your family really has the full spectrum of criminal activity covered, don't you?"

"Necklace? And what's this about criminal activity?" he asked skeptically, pausing to sip.

"So you don't deny the stalking?"

"Why don't we start from the beginning."

"Why don't *you* ask Victor?" Her tone was sharp, like a dagger poised in the air.

He set his cup down. "How do you know Victor's name?"

"My necklace and passport were stolen, and I have proof he was involved."

Oliver's thoughts accelerated to fill in the gaps of what she was and everything she wasn't. Her necklace was stolen, and she knew Victor's name and, ostensibly, his criminal history. He briefly recalled his cousin's commentary about the pendant she'd been wearing.

"Why don't we start with a name," asked Oliver, attempting to de-escalate. "What's your name?"

"You don't seem surprised." She studied him.

Oliver thought of Victor at seventeen and at twenty two, all the ways his cousin had chosen a course that led to his self-destruction.

"Why don't we sit?" He gestured to an empty booth.

He heard a slight grumble from her stomach, which she attempted to quiet with a palm. Oliver slid into one side of an empty booth, a gold lamp swaying in small movements with the forward motion of the train. Hesitating, she slid into the opposite side of the booth. She slid aside the small green vase filled with flowers.

"Fine. I'll only sit and eat because I haven't since Rome. But I'm serious about getting answers."

"I believe you."

A different attendant arrived and set down two menus alongside two small glasses of water. He met her gaze over the white-clothed table. While it was clear her anger hadn't fully dissipated, perhaps her hunger was neutral ground for them to stand on.

"The lamb, please," she said.

"The cod. Thank you." Oliver handed over the menu. He began reaching into his wallet.

"You seem very different from your cousin," said Lucia with suspicion.

"I've never been arrested before, which is a start."

She scoffed. "Maybe you've just never been caught—"

He placed his badge on the table. She flipped it rapidly to face her.

"That would be a true work hazard, considering I'm a detective."

Within the fold of thin, black leather, his name was displayed above a series of numbers. The words *Swedish Police Authority* were inscribed on his identification card. Lucia's head bowed over the table, reading slowly before lifting her eyes. There was a lingering trace of wariness, though now it was paired with deepened curiosity.

"My name is Lucia."

"Your name is interesting," said Oliver, who watched her eyes trace the details of his badge. "Is it Spanish?"

"Yeah, my father is from Madrid—" Lucia halted, eyes darting up from his badge. "Never mind about my father." She slid his identification card to him across the table.

"You seem like you want to ask me something."

"Not a question," clarified Lucia. "It's that you ... don't *look* like a detective."

"What are we supposed to look like?" Oliver asked as he tried not to laugh. He leaned forward on his forearms across the table, fingers interlaced.

"I take it back," said Lucia, eyeing his posture. "You seem like you have endurance for a six-hour interrogation."

"That is oddly specific." A small smile drew up the corner of his mouth before he could stop himself. Just then, their entrees arrived, and Lucia excused herself to the bathroom. When she returned a few minutes later, both plates were still untouched. She took her seat.

"You could have started without me."

"I'm in no hurry," said Oliver. "It's a long train ride home."

"So ..." Lucia began unrolling silverware from a cloth napkin. "You have an impressive decade-long career as a detective sergeant. Did you always want to work at the Swedish Police Authority in Stockholm?"

With an imperceptible pause, he finished the bite off his fork. "You got this all from a trip to the lavatory?"

"Something like that," said Lucia guardedly. Her tone was stitched together with unflinching resolve. It reminded him of the first time he'd seen her in Rome. She seemed to be the same person everywhere she went. Uncertain of where and how she obtained information about him, it seemed the verification of his identity relaxed her marginally.

Oliver chewed for a moment before setting his fork down. "Will you tell me what you think happened with Victor and your necklace?"

"The facts," began Lucia as her fingers enumerated. "One, a necklace was given to me by my mother. Two, I was wearing it yesterday when I ran into you and Victor, which he commented on. Three, someone broke into my hotel room last night and stole it."

"Were you in the room?" asked Oliver.

"I was in the shower and heard him leave. I tried to catch up before he got too far. Down the hall from my room, I discovered a ticket and credit card receipt, both of which matched identically with a last name and card number. I might also add, one of the receipts was from the same bar I also happened to be at. Which leads me to believe he followed me. So we've got burglary *and* stalking."

"That was from our first night in Rome," said Oliver, a memory of a bright nightclub pulsing in his head. "But I'm not sure how he could have. I was with him practically the entire time."

"All some people need is opportunity." She dropped her fork, the metal clanging against the plate. "I know for a fact the receipts belong to him, which is how I found out his name. And doesn't he have a history of this?"

"Victor is a lot of things, but I've never known him to be aggressive toward women like that." He leaned in the booth, mentally working through the merits of her points. "What did the police say when you filed a report?"

"If they had been helpful, I wouldn't be here sitting across from you."

Oliver cocked his head. "How did you find his address in Stockholm?"

"Through an international connection," Lucia hedged, shifting in her seat.

"Impressive *and* concerning."

They sat in silence as the train car pushed forward through the countryside. He was struck with a sudden loss of appetite from the conversation and placed his napkin on the table.

"Wait—" said Oliver, "but are you on your way to Stockholm?"

She shifted her gaze away without answering.

"That's a bit bold, isn't it? Going alone to confront a man you think might've robbed you?"

She went pale. "You make him sound dangerous."

Witnessing his cousin's emotional nature was one thing. Her accusation brought to light what he already knew, having been witness to Victor's mercurial moods. Was theft a way to patch over some unspoken loneliness? Or greed? As if some empty space inside of Victor could only be filled by something or someone else?

"As a general rule in my line of work," said Oliver. "It's always a good idea to involve the authorities instead of playing detective."

"That's exactly what I did in Rome, and it's the plan for Stockholm." Her voice was laced with impatience. "I already promised

Si—a friend in New York that I wouldn't confront Victor myself. I won't. But I refuse to be idle while your cousin potentially tries to sell that necklace."

An attendant came by just then, and Oliver pulled out his wallet to put his credit card down.

"If you didn't follow me and you weren't aware of what Victor did—how are we here right now?" asked Lucia.

"You mean on this train at the same time?"

"Yes," said Lucia with an unspoken tone of *obviously*.

"I was only in Rome for a week. We went our separate ways right after our encounter with you. I took a late train out of Rome for work next week."

With her eyes focused out the window, Oliver followed her gaze. They passed a lake, clear and glimmering from the sun that hung lower than when they'd sat to eat.

"What's your plan?" asked Oliver.

"So you can warn Victor?" She lowered her water glass from her lips. "No."

"Whether you believe me or not, I do want to help you," responded Oliver.

An announcement from overhead flooded the train car, informing passengers the brief stop into Amsterdam was ten minutes away. She ran her hands through her hair in exasperation. "I am desperate to get my belongings. I plan to file a report in Stockholm, which should bring a bit more success than it did in Italy. I don't want that necklace to end up on the black market."

Oliver recalled a case from a few years back involving the Swedish royal family. They'd expressed concern about the very same thing. He and his team had been able to recover one of the items, but security was heightened to prevent something from happening again. He knew that once something reached the black market, it was nearly impossible to track it down.

"I presume the police in your country will take care of the rest," said Lucia. In that second, her cell phone rang from the outer pocket of her bag. Briefly, she viewed the screen before answering.

"Simon?" she answered. Turning her profile, she pressed the phone to her ear. "Wait, wait—what are you saying?"

"When?" A portrait of long dark curls splayed across her back. Her shoulders stiffened before whirling to the window of the train. "Tell him thanks again. I *really* don't want to know the details of this favor he owed you." The train began to slow, not far from pulling up to the station.

"Let's go," said Lucia. She pushed away at the booth. A few paces ahead, she whirled to find Oliver still sitting. "Are you coming?"

"Despite what Americans might think," said Oliver, "not all European cities are alike. We haven't reached Sweden yet."

Lucia whirled frantically to the doors where passengers were preparing to disembark. She placed her palms on the surface of the table and stared Oliver right in the eyes. "I know where I am. Victor is here and I need you to come to Amsterdam with me."

CHAPTER THIRTEEN

ROME

A thousand miles away, Officer Costa was shuffling paperwork. The *questura* was beginning to empty out as the lunch hour neared. It only compounded his bitterness to continue working on the hotel case. His colleague, Ivan, set a small cup of espresso at Costa's desk. With a square jaw and a better work ethic, he irritated Costa the most. Costa jutted his chin toward a desk across the room.

"Why don't you go sit over there."

Moving to sit in the chair on the other side of Costa's desk, Ivan raised the cup from its small plate and took a sip.

"Do you always wake up in a sour mood, or is it just this week?" asked Ivan as he crossed his legs.

Costa leaned in his chair. "I've been assigned to handle an errant case. A complete waste of my time."

"Oh? Because police work is so beneath you?" asked Ivan with a chuckle.

"An American woman is claiming a robbery. There's been no real evidence, and the items in question include a valuable and apparently rare heirloom."

"Anything else missing?" asked Ivan, reaching for the report.

"Her passport," said Costa. "Seems more like insurance fraud though. She reeked of money."

"What do you mean?" Ivan continued reading the document in his hand.

Costa waved a hand dismissively. "There's no proof of her having brought the necklace with her to Rome."

"What about surveillance?"

"Out of service."

Ivan gave his full attention. "Which hotel?"

"The *Fontana Blu*. Why?"

"What kind of necklace?" Ivan leaned forward.

"If you have so many questions, why don't *you* take the case?" Irritation creased in visible lines between Costa's brows.

Ivan merely pursed his lips before taking another sip of espresso. With an exaggerated sigh, Costa leaned over to pull a cabinet drawer open, removing a folder. He turned the file to show Ivan a color photo Lucia had emailed him that morning. A close-up of a woman in her fifties smiling at the camera, the necklace perfectly framed within the photo.

"A gold and jade necklace. Apparently, her mother's, which the victim inherited after she passed away recently."

Sympathy shone from Ivan's expression, who held the picture closer. "Unfortunate that the hotel cameras weren't operational. It actually reminds me of another case. A German woman, visiting for the week who was staying near the *Colosseo*."

"What happened in the case?"

"Well, that's just the thing," said Ivan intently. "Another woman from Morroco filed a report with me that her ruby earrings and passport had been stolen from her hotel room. The German woman claimed her diamond bracelet was stolen while she was on the metro. Just the other day, I heard about another similar case involving another tourist whose diamond ring was stolen. It might be a co-incidence, but something tells me it's something else."

Slow realization crept up on Costa. "You think someone is targeting tourists and robbing them of their identification and jewelry?"

"These aren't just thefts; they're high-price items stolen from foreigners. The theft of the passports could be personal, or it could be identity-targeted acts," said Ivan. "By the time they get back to their country, there's enough distance. Enough time passes that the culprit is long gone before an investigation really takes place. It's just how it is, but if someone knew this, it would work to their benefit."

Ivan grabbed his espresso cup. He motioned to Costa with his head in the direction of his desk.

"Who else has similar cases?" asked Costa, pushing himself out of the chair. He followed Ivan, shuffling from foot-to-foot in his black boots, impatient.

"I could always find out," said Ivan.

"All these thefts," said Costa. "Do you think they've been done by the same person?"

"Could be. See for yourself," said Ivan, pointing to his computer screen.

All Costa saw was a blurred image of a figure wearing a ball cap near the exit of a train. "That's it?"

"Yet, it is still more than what you started with."

Costa winced, his face turning slightly red. "I only meant ..."

Ivan leaned against the desk, folding his hands in front of him. Clearing his throat, Costa said, "I appreciate you sharing this with me. What do you think this means?"

"The CCTV footage is shit, but it's something to go on. By the look of it, it's a man under that hat, about 150 centimeters tall. It appears as if he knows where to avoid being seen by the camera. The theft of luxury jewelry and passports in the same area of Rome within a few days of each other? It doesn't seem entirely accidental," said Ivan. He leaned his hands behind his head. "I can't say I'm a believer of coincidences. And now a third at a nearby hotel?"

The figure was obscured and unclear through the static on the screen. Rome was Costa's city, and his protectiveness, while solipsistic, arrived with a vengeance. "I believe I'll be giving the hotel manager at *Fontana Blu* another call.

Chapter Fourteen

Amsterdam

"Amsterdam has a funny sense of humor about summer," said Lucia.

Across the table, he took a sip from a glass of water. After trekking from the train station, they'd ducked into a small cafe by a canal to escape the cold winds. May in Amsterdam wasn't quite what she'd thought it would be.

"If you think this is cold, you should spend time in Sweden," said Oliver with a grin.

"Only a man who lives in the tundra would say that," replied Lucia.

"Here," Oliver slid a palm-sized leather-bound menu across the table. "Order something to drink. We both could use it."

"Drinking is for celebration. I am *not* celebrating." Lucia groaned, laying her forehead in the crook of her arm. "We were so close to finding Victor here. How did we just miss him?"

The only way she'd been able to persuade Oliver to disembark the train was to tell him about Simon. She had information on Victor's flight to Amsterdam, as verified by a card transaction made the day before. A second call delivered the bad news: a latent notification reflected Victor's name in the system for a flight to Berlin, which had departed an hour before their arrival in the city center of Amsterdam. Since the robbery in Rome, it was as if she could only grasp tendrils of cataclysmic moments within time. Fear slowly spun her in circles, dizzying her with ominous fortune-telling. How could she *not* regard the loss of her mother's necklace as confirmation that it didn't belong to her in the first place?

Oliver gestured to the waiter, holding up two fingers. "Yes, hello. I'd like a gin and tonic. Lucia?"

Ambivalent to what she drank, she closed the menu. "One for me as well."

Beyond the cafe doors, cyclists rode past, their wheels spinning beneath a clear sky. Two glasses were placed on the table, and Lucia sat in her chair as the waiter walked away. Blinking, she took in their setting. Though small, the cafe had high ceilings. A red striped rug lay beneath her feet. Books were stacked artfully on shelves and light filled up the corners of the shop from the wide front window. Their table was only a few feet from the door; she shivered each time someone walked in.

"Perhaps we should consider an alternative plan," said Oliver. "If I contact Victor, I can meet him somewhere and talk to him in person."

"He could deny any involvement in stealing my necklace," countered Lucia. "Bringing my knowledge of him to his attention could have irreversible consequences." She turned her gaze toward the view outside. "I'm—desperate for it not to be sold."

Oliver watched her, a sympathetic expression on his face.

"Don't do that," said Lucia with a finger pointing at his chest.

"I only want to help. It is an option to call him, that's all I'm saying. It's not a terrible idea."

"It is," said Lucia adamantly. "Because you strike me as a terrible and unpracticed liar."

A smile hooked his mouth at the corner, the first she'd seen. It quickly disappeared as he placed both palms on the table, turning them until his fingers laced together. His lack of defensiveness, his willingness to help her, and the intensity of his blue eyes were really starting to piss her off.

He slid the second glass in her direction. "Gin or water, your choice. But I think you should drink something."

She reached for the glass and took a sip. It was satisfying but did not soothe the unsettled feeling in her stomach. She'd dragged them off the train with nothing beyond the hope of finding both Victor and her mother's necklace. The entire circumstance she'd put herself in—both of them—was miserable.

"It's getting late," said Lucia. "I ... I suppose we should find a place to stay for the evening. The last time I showered was two countries ago."

"I agree." He looked up briefly before returning to his phone. "About accommodations, not the shower."

She took another sip, nudging a toe against her leather luggage. Across the street, elm trees were bursting to life with blooming green leaves, their limbs stretched skyward. Pedestrians made their way through the doors of a nearby market. Oliver set his phone down on the table.

"It's all set," said Oliver. He gestured to the waiter. "I'll take care of the bill and we can head to the hotel. Check-in is already available."

"What?" Lucia narrowed her eyes.

"Two rooms at a decent hotel in the nearby art district. Feel welcome to forward yourself the reservation email." He slid his phone toward her.

She scrolled through the page. Glancing at him, she typed in her email. They both heard the chime notification from her phone. She immediately sent it to Adeline and Simon with a brief note, *I'll explain later.* "Thanks. I'll grab a cab." She felt better assured of her safety.

When they arrived by taxi at the hotel, Oliver pushed the door open for her, moving to grab the luggage in the trunk. At the concierge desk, Oliver verified the reservation he'd made.

"Here you are, sir. I have provided two key cards, one for yourself and one for your wife."

Lucia's attention, which had been fixated on the hotel's vaulted ceilings, whipped to the male concierge.

"He's *not* my husband," she said with a forceful shake of her head.

"What she said—she's not my husband either," said Oliver.

Lucia rolled her eyes and reached for the key cards. "We'll take these."

"Seventh floor." The concierge cleared his throat behind them. "Please enjoy your stay."

Oliver responded in a language she assumed was Dutch. They stepped into an empty elevator. The small hum of passing floors filled the space as she handed him the card to his room. She gave him a curious side-eye. "How many languages do you speak?"

"Why do you ask?"

"Because I'm nosy."

"No," said Oliver with a smirk, "something tells me you're competitive."

"Those detective skills are really something," said Lucia. Once on the seventh floor, carpet underfoot muted their steps down the hall.

"I speak four languages," said Oliver. "Not that it matters."

"Of course you do," Lucia muttered.

Oliver pointedly ignored her as he glanced at room numbers displayed on each wall. He paused in front of a door, moving his bag over his shoulder before turning to her. 708 appeared on a small frame.

"How can I send you money for the room?" she asked.

"No need," said Oliver, his eyes never leaving hers. He silently turned the key card over in his hands, his eyes on hers.

Since running into him on the train, he didn't seem to say much. It made her almost self-conscious of her words. Was his quiet nature a tactic to unsettle her? Or was it just who he was, saying what he meant and meaning what he said, if he made the effort to open his mouth in the first place? As she scanned the key card against the door, Oliver helped push the door open, giving her space to walk through. He stood in the hall. Lucia set her luggage down and turned to him. An electric current of something between them sent a shiver down her arms. A stillness of nature's chemistry. It would be so much easier if he were hideous, thought Lucia.

"Are you hungry?" asked Lucia before she could stop herself.

Don't be stupid don't be stupid.

"I could eat. Are you?"

"Famished," said Lucia honestly.

"There's always room service since it's getting late," he suggested. "I'm not sure how late restaurants are open."

"Yes ... or," Lucia cleared her throat, "we could get a proper meal. I spotted a restaurant in the hotel downstairs."

"A proper dinner it is," said Oliver, as if surprising himself. "I'll meet you downstairs in a half an hour."

Oliver gave a polite nod, but she detected something soft underneath his words. She closed the door of her room, but in her last view of him, Lucia detected curiosity in his expression and something else. Something deeper.

***

Lucia stood in front of a full-length mirror in her suite. Her hair had been in a top knot for the last few hours, and she pulled it loose, running a hand through it and lightly massaging out her scalp.

The last twenty four hours began to sink in. She gave a long exhale. Sitting on the bed, Lucia placed her palms behind her. The duvet cover was a soft cotton beneath her hands. Easing down, she lay on her side. The window curtains were closed. In the quiet of the room, she could gather her thoughts.

There was so much to sort through. There was monetary value in the necklace, of course, but why would Victor take the other two things? What would he gain by also stealing her passport and dress? Did he grab it in a hurry or to humiliate? Was it revenge for his damaged book? It certainly felt personal. She considered her first impression of him. To her, he seemed like a man led by ego. Most people driven by ego couldn't be trusted with objective truths about themselves.

She went to the floor to retrieve her luggage. Opening one end of her suitcase, she began to sort through folded clothes of silk and wool. She'd always wanted to visit Amsterdam but had chosen other places to visit instead. Maybe in another life, she could be here, freely stumbling through alleyways and canals, drunk off the magical quality of the city. It occurred to her that she hadn't messaged Adeline since running into Victor and Oliver in Rome and decided to call. Checking the last message in their chat, she saw the picture of them as kids Adeline had sent. The uninhibited grins of their younger selves smiled back at her.

"I was just thinking of you," said Adeline by way of greeting. "What was the email you sent me and Si?"

"It's a long story. I'm not calling you too early, am I?"

"Lucia, I hate to be the one to remind you," said Adeline with a laugh, "but you're terrible with numbers. It's not even three in the afternoon."

"Right. I knew that," her eyes shuttered closed. She leaned her head against the wall. "It makes sense now when I think about Simon's call earlier."

"We had an ongoing bet on who you would contact first. I'm disappointed to hear you love me less," said Adeline with a distracted pout. Lucia could hear her son Theo singing off-key.

"It wasn't like that. I needed his help with something."

"I hope you aren't upset that I told your dad that you left for Italy. He was worried after the will reading and—"

"Addy, someone broke into my hotel room in Rome."

"Someone did *what*?" Lucia could practically see Adeline's hands gesturing in the air. "Oh my god—are you okay? What happened?"

Lucia explained everything, sharing every detail of the interaction she'd had in Rome with Victor and Oliver. Of finding the train tickets. The *polizia*. Getting help from Lorenzo with Simon's help. Admitting to her that she had withheld her plan of traveling to Stockholm from Simon. Running into Oliver on the train. Lastly: stranded in Amsterdam without a plan.

"Let me make sure I understand this ... The man you are attempting to track through Europeno, let me rephrase: the man *related* to the guy who stole your mother's necklace is Swedish law enforcement and wants to help you? Is he attractive? I bet he's hot."

"Is that all you think about?" Lucia hung her head with a weak laugh.

"Of course not. But I also think this would make an excellent spin-off for *CSI: International*. I can see it already—'*Based on a true story*,'" intoned Adeline. "Just, you know, please don't get murdered."

"I was able to confirm Oliver's identity, and you both have my hotel information. My gut instinct also says Oliver can be trusted," said Lucia.

"How did you get Simon to give you information about Oliver without telling him you were on a train to Stockholm?"

"I, erm, said I'd found more documentation related to Victor." Lucia cleared her throat. Pushing herself off the floor, she walked to the window. With one hand, she pulled aside the curtain. In the twenty minutes she'd been on the phone, the setting sun had turned its golden tint eastward on Amsterdam.

"Simon's going to be so worried when he finds out," Adeline pointed out. "Lucia, you should tell him."

"I know, and I will," Lucia promised. "I'll tell him everything tonight."

"Good. Does your dad know where you are?"

"He mentioned you'd told him about my trip to Italy. I just ... I don't know what to say," admitted Lucia. "I'm sure Corinne told you what a dumpster fire the meeting was before I left."

"She did ... though I believe she called it something else."

"Something more polite than a fucking disaster?"

"She wants what I want, which is for you to be okay." Adeline seemed to choose her words carefully. "I can see your mother in a way even my mother can't. Your mom has always been a bit … cold. Removed. What she said the last time you saw her was horrible. I guess that's why I'm … "

"You're what?"

"Surprised."

"At which part: the burglary or my fleeing to Rome?"

"I suppose I'm surprised you wore the necklace at all," Adeline said gently.

"I never gave thought to that necklace other than the fact that it belonged to her." Lucia felt the tidal wave of emotion swell in her belly, rising up. She placed the heel of her left hand against her chest. "Even at the will reading, I tried to give it back to my dad. He was convinced she wanted me to have it. Why did she leave me responsible for this—this thing? She never even called me to tell me she was sick." Bitterness lodged itself in her throat. Since the funeral, a cavernous space inside her, so large and hollow, threatened to swallow her whole. Tears pricked at the corners of her eyes, but she refused to shed them. They were quiet, decades of friendship bridged between them despite the silence. Adeline's son was murmuring still, singing something about the tops of strawberries and train cars.

"Before she died," whispered Lucia, "I'd started to forget the sound of her voice. I could go days without remembering it. I shouldn't care about this necklace. I never saw it as mine, yet now that it's gone, the void of it … it's like … "

"What is it like?"

"Losing the necklace is like losing her as a mother again. I don't know if I can survive that twice."

CHAPTER FIFTEEN

A few doors down from Lucia's room, Oliver was pacing in his.

What the hell have you done, Victor?

Splashing cold water on his face, Oliver heard his phone ring in the other room. His sister's name displayed on the screen.

"Linnea."

"Why does it always sound like I'm in trouble when you answer? *I'm* the eldest."

"That's just how I talk," said Oliver, patting his face with a small hand towel. He could hear his nieces playing.

"Are you on your way back from Rome?"

By answering Linnea's call, Oliver had known he'd be confronting this exact question and everything that came along with it. He hesitated.

"Well, don't talk all at once," teased Linnea.

"I left for Stockholm yesterday. I'm in Amsterdam now."

"Oh?" she asked with surprise. "I didn't realize you were going there. What's in Amsterdam?"

"Victor seems to be involved in something big." Oliver plunged into the cold waters of honesty. "Maybe even something quite unpleasantly illegal. I'm trying to find out more information."

He heard her whisper to her daughters to play in the other room. She began hissing a plethora of slurs in Swedish. Grimacing a little, he held the phone away from his ear. "An official investigation?"

"It's not associated with the Swedish Police Authority," replied Oliver.

"As in currently or inevitably?" asked Linnea without humor.

"Until I talk to Victor, the information is really on a need-to-know basis."

"So he doesn't know that you know ... whatever it is that you know."

"Correct."

"Is he trying to put our aunt into an early grave?" asked Linnea as she let out a heavy sigh. In a variety of different ways, he'd heard some semblance of this remark over the years.

"I know you get along with him. I truly thought he was doing much better with that job at the framer's shop. He's even made different kinds of friends than he usually keeps around," Linnea conceded. "But if Victor has done something illegal again, this could have lifelong consequences. For everyone."

Oliver sat at the edge of the bed. He could hear Linnea walking through her house, the sound of her picking up small toys.

"For now, Lin, keep the Victor thing to yourself until I know more."

"Fine. I can do that."

At the sound of something crashing, her words clipped off to check on the girls, whom he could hear giggling, reassuring everyone they were fine. Linnea's daughters shouted with glee through the phone.

"Aaron just walked in."

Oliver could hear his brother-in-law say something. Linnea said, "He says 'hello,' but I wish he'd simply ignore you like I do."

"You called me," said Oliver with a laugh.

"I need to go. We have to put the girls down."

"A bit dark, Lin; they're just innocent children."

"Always a surprise, you are." His sister gave a quick laugh before hanging up. He set the phone beside him on the bed. With curtains wide open, the room had slowly grown darker from the sunset. He tried to reconcile how the cousin he cared for could have broken into Lucia's hotel room. In the past few years, Victor had seemed to be making improvements to his life, beyond the job and the friends.

So much of his work required combing through the past. For any of his active cases, inspecting personal history was the starting point. The past always gave crucial information for the present, no matter how much someone wanted to leave it behind. He couldn't see his cousin's life without thinking about the death of Victor's father. Several years before, Oliver had been the one to pick up Victor from jail the day he was released. Victor had been filled with intense shame. Oliver had seen the way it darkened his features. But Victor had always been a bit intemperate, had always struggled with his inclination for risk-taking. How could Victor really be so reckless again?

Oliver thought he'd changed—but what if self-destruction was a cliff's edge on which Victor would always stand?

He grappled with the blade of forgiveness and guilt. Both cleaved him open with uncertainty and doubt. But life could change in an instant. Oliver knew it could have been his father, his own family, splintered apart. The only difference is that it had happened to Victor.

***

Stockholm, Sweden, Nineteen years earlier

"What the hell happened?"

Oliver and Victor sat in a park, two fifteen-year-olds procrastinating the walk home from school. From Victor's brief text—*park, fourteen o'clock*, and nothing else—Oliver knew it was something serious.

"It started with a big argument about curfew. I was only twenty minutes late. You know how he is, always yelling, but this time, I couldn't take it anymore. He seemed more angry than usual. I thought maybe it was work or a fight with my mother or something," said Victor as he smashed an empty soda can against the ground. "I yelled back and called him by his first name just to spite him. And he seemed ready for it. He told me that if I'm old enough to call him

Anders, I'm old enough to know I was an accident. That life would have been much, much easier with just the two of them." Victor swallowed, his hands across his knees.

"He said that?" Oliver was baffled. "Where was Aunt Hanna?"

At the mention of his mother, Victor lifted his head. "She wasn't around. I tried to tell her when she got home last night, but you know she always sides with him. She said it's hard to trust my 'narrative of events' given that I've been dishonest before," said Victor, lifting his hands to make air quotes. "I know she'll never leave him, but he's kind of the worst."

"That's ... horrible," said Oliver. He could never imagine his father saying half the things he'd heard his uncle say to Victor.

"You're the only one who ever believes me," said Victor. He lifted his eyes up at Oliver.

Oliver had witnessed his cousin embellish certain parts of his stories over the years or paint a picture of something into a far more exaggerated version than the original. But he'd never heard Victor fabricate something from nothing. He'd once overheard his parents talk about a fight Victor's parents had and its volatile nature. Breaking up and getting back together, over and over. There was always a sense that there was more to his uncle beyond his charming presentation for public consumption. It seemed entirely plausible to Oliver that Anders was not only indifferent to Victor but cruel.

His cousin pushed himself off the ground where they sat, glancing at his phone. Flipping the screen to Oliver, he nodded and stood. Though they'd each skipped the last class of the day, they'd need to start walking to arrive home around the usual time. Oliver's flat was less than a kilometer from Victor's, so they'd often walk in the same direction. On the sidewalk, occasional conversations at cafes and passing cars were the only sounds between them. A street away from Victor's, Oliver asked, "What if I had my mom talk to Aunt Hanna?"

Victor's laugh broke in half at Oliver's expression. "No way," said Victor with a shake of his head. "That would get me into worse trouble. I would never hear the end of it."

Together, they reached the door to Victor's flat. Oliver snapped his fingers, his navy pack sliding down his arm at the motion.

"I just realized I left my biology book at yours."

A hesitant groove deepend on Victor's face. "If you make it quick, you can come up and get it. My dad won't be home from work yet."

"I will," said Oliver with a nod. Victor's worry meant the argument must've been pretty bad the night before.

They walked through the entrance of the apartment building, taking a spiral set of stairs to Victor's front door. As they walked in, Victor tossed his bag onto one of the sofas in the TV room. The blinds were partially open, throwing fragmented lines of shadows and light across the floor.

Victor walked into the kitchen without bothering to turn on the light. Fluorescent white spilled across the wood floor as he opened the fridge.

"I'm going to grab the book from your room," said Oliver. Searching the surface of Victor's desk, he heard his aunt's voice in the other room. Hanna was facing the kitchen as Oliver waved from the door frame.

"Did you just get home from school? Hi, Oliver."

"Hi, Aunt Hanna. I'm just grabbing a book I forgot the other day."

"I'm off to dinner with Anders. You should probably head home when you can. Victor's a bit housebound, unfortunately," she said. She began swapping jackets from the coat rack.

Oliver nodded, unzipping his bag as three sharp knocks rapped on the front door. She pulled it open, and two uniformed officers filled the entrance.

"Yes?" asked Hanna. "What's this about?"

From the room, Oliver couldn't hear much. He held the textbook on its spine as he tentatively stepped outside Victor's room.

"That's my husband," said Hanna, "but he isn't here. I'm meeting him at a restaurant for dinner."

Pieces of the conversation from the officers were coming in waves, their voices so soft Oliver could only hear every other word. "Murdered ... between 12:45 and 13:30 ... We're so sorry."

His aunt gasped, gripping the door frame. "You have the wrong Anders Hedlund," said Hanna forcefully. "I spoke with him earlier. He's meeting me for dinner."

The officers exchanged a look between them. "Do you recognize this woman?" asked one of them. He pulled out a small photo from his interior jacket pocket. Each word was staccato.

With a sharp inhale, Hanna stood, her hands gripping each arm.

"I think she's a colleague. What does she have to do with my husband?"

"Unfortunately," said the tallest officer, "they've been having an affair, and her husband confronted them with a knife. We have him in custody; he confessed at the scene of the crime." The officer's hair was so short Oliver could see his pink scalp beneath the hallway lights. "There were no survivors."

Oliver took a step closer, swiveling to Victor, whose eyes were on his mother. Hanna bent at the waist, two hands across her face. Her body turned toward the doorknob, leaning on it for support. In profile, her mouth formed a silent cry. Within the flat, the shock was palpable. Hanna had begun to make soft, keening sounds into her hands.

"We understand this is very difficult, Mrs. Hedlund," said the second officer. "The body will need to be identified—" he stopped as Hanna began hyperventilating. He noticed Oliver in his direct line of sight. "I'm so sorry. Could we please escort you both to the morgue?"

"I'm—I'm not," Oliver clumsily stepped over words to find the right ones. "He's—he was my uncle—"

Before Hanna's knees could lower to meet the floor, before Victor could rush to wrap his arms around her and calmly declare he would be the one to identify his father's body, Oliver noticed desperate disbelief written on his cousin's face. A disbelief that would unspool itself around their family for years to come. Seized between the worst news of his life and himself, Victor's anguish and shock cast outward, his face shrouded in partial shadow. He looked so young just then, as if towed into a sudden and forceful slipstream with no instructions of how to keep from drowning.

Chapter Sixteen

Not an hour later, Lucia and Oliver were sitting across from each other in the hotel restaurant.

The dining room was decorated with sleek surfaces and gold frames filled with splashy art. The space was something between Art Deco and mid-century modern. Behind the bar, tiers of liquor bottles shined on glass shelves. Crown molding gave a decadent nod to history. Its opulent, sweeping interior drew eyes to three walls of windows. Above them, the evening sky peered down through a skylight.

Conversations from patrons only traveled as far as the next table. There was a pleasant chime of keys on the piano by a woman who sat framed between floor-to-ceiling curtains. Dim lights set the mood of a chilly night in May. Engrossed, Lucia's slender arms were exposed in motion from the silk sleeves of her dress.

"This is far fancier than I'd anticipated," said Lucia, glancing at him before turning to watch the piano player. "I was picturing cheeseburgers and fries."

"I don't bother eating in public unless it's at least three courses," joked Oliver with the menu in his hands.

"I hadn't realized Swedish detectives had a thing for fine dining," said Lucia, a wry smile sneaking through.

"I wouldn't know," said Oliver.

"Because you're not Swedish, or you're not a detective?" Lucia bit back a grin.

His only response was a sardonic look that made her chuckle.

A waiter arrived to take their orders. When the waiter turned to her, Lucia ordered white wine mussels and handed over the menu. Oliver's eyes held hers as he took a sip of water. She could see the shape of his arms through his shirt as he set down the glass.

Something fluttery and weighted in the center of her took shape. When it was just them in silence, it gnawed at her. Growing up, she'd always hated long stretches of silence with her mother. Pressing a hand flat atop her dress, she tried to smooth it out of restlessness. Or nervousness. Looking away from Oliver and out to the rest of the room, she couldn't be sure.

"You have a way of going somewhere and turning it off very suddenly," commented Oliver, interrupting her thoughts. "Does this happen often?"

"Are you profiling me?" asked Lucia half-seriously.

"As if you haven't been doing the same since we met," he gave a grin.

Heat from her neck rose to her cheeks. The blue of his eyes reminded her of a documentary she'd seen once about Alaska in the winter. They were the same shade of blue as water when it solidified in the Arctic, frozen for long periods of time.

"I was thinking of my mother," said Lucia. *Why are you telling this to someone you just met?*

"I imagine you were quite close, given the lengths you're going to to find the necklace," commented Oliver.

"I would never say that."

"Oh?" Oliver gave a tilt of his head.

"She was ... we were ... " she reached for the right words. "Very different people. Her career came first, and she was always a bit oblivious to others unless they directly affected her. We hadn't been in contact for years when she died."

Oliver's glass of water that had been halfway to his lips froze mid-air. "She passed away recently?"

"A week ago, more or less," said Lucia, averting her eyes as her hands lightly tapped the stem of her glass. "But I was told she'd been sick for a while."

The waiter appeared and began pouring white wine. Lucia barely registered the year and region explained to her, nor paid much attention when the waiter disappeared again.

"Do you want to talk about it?" His gaze was warm in the flickering candlelight.

"I actually don't know much about it other than it was a rare form of cancer," said Lucia, staring into her wine. "I didn't even know."

Oliver paused. "She didn't tell you?"

"She did not."

"How ... complicated that she took that from you." He seemed to be thinking deeply. "And herself."

His words shook loose a heartache in her that she wanted to keep buried.

"What was her name?" asked Oliver.

"Rowan." Her eyes seared with small blinks. "Her name was Rowan."

"What do you think her opinion would be about your decision to trek through Europe for her necklace after all those years of not speaking?" asked Oliver.

"If you had asked me a few weeks ago, I would have been shocked to even have the necklace. Now, maybe ..." Lucia craned her neck toward the skylight, the black of night above them. "I think her reaction might surprise me. *I'm* surprised to be here. She used to travel here a lot and loves—loved this city."

"She sounds like she was a really perplexing person."

"Seems to run in our families," noted Lucia. Empathy glimmered in her thinking of his career as a detective and being related to someone so indifferent to the law.

Her dysfunctional relationship with Rowan showed her what it was like having a family member you felt compelled to apologize for. In intimate relationships, she'd always become wrapped up in the potential of people, ignoring the reality of who they were because she hoped for something different. She'd often loved people who could never live up to an idealized version of who she wanted them to be. Maybe she'd been selfish like her mother, in a different way.

When the food arrived, it offered a distraction that released a little bit of tension in her chest. The steaming mussels in front of her smelled delicious. White wine sauce saturated half-open shells. Oliver raised his glass by its stem.

"To exceeding expectations. This is far better than room service."

"So generous of you to tolerate a one-course meal with a simple peasant like me," said Lucia, unable to hide a smile.

"If someone has to do it, it should be me." Light etchings of crow's feet formed at the corners of his eyes.

As the night unwound over their meal, conversation weaved around safer topics. Oliver told her about growing up in Stockholm. About close friends who had moved from Turkey and his brother-in-law from Ethiopia, all of whom made him want to travel, and see the world differently than the rest of his peers. Lucia made a mental note of the way he mentioned his two sisters, one a scientist and the other an architect.

She considered asking him why he'd pursued law enforcement, but something told her the reason was deeply personal. It was apparent to her his disposition, thorough and detailed, seemed fitted for it.

When New York came up, she offered stories of growing up with Adeline and the mischief they'd get into by sneaking out to Washington Square Park on hot summer nights to dip their feet in the fountain. Perhaps for the first time in a very long time, the evening felt soft, easy. She wasted none of the white sauce at the end of her fork—or the wine. Lucia enjoyed herself despite the unbelievable events that had led her there.

Partway through the conversation, Oliver's phone rang. At the sound, he checked the screen. Frowning, he raised his eyes to hers, answering.

"Victor?"

CHAPTER SEVENTEEN

"Hej, Oliver!"

Victor's voice came through the phone, dissonant to the quiet murmur of the restaurant. Oliver could see mixed emotions flicker across Lucia's eyes.

"I can't talk long," said Victor in Swedish, "but I can't seem to find my credit card. Do you remember seeing it?"

"Not sure. Maybe the last time was at the cafe in Rome?"

Lucia gripped her dinner fork.

"Ah, that damn espresso … " muttered Victor. "I'll need to cancel my card then. I should have enough cash on hand for now. "

"Will it be enough for the final leg of your trip?"

"It should be. I'm in Berlin now to meet with the buyer in the morning, but I won't be able to deposit the check until I get home."

"How is Berlin?" Oliver chose his words carefully.

"Soggy. It's been raining since I got here. Not quite like Ams—"

Victor was cut off by a loud ambulance on his end of the call. Oliver could barely hear a thing.

"So fucking loud," said Victor, his voice rising above the siren.

Once it quieted, regular street din returned in the background.

"Will I see you in a few days?" asked Oliver. Waitstaff passed, topping off half-filled water glasses.

"In Stockholm? Ah, maybe a few more days—I've decided to take a detour."

He waited a beat in case Victor offered any more information before asking, "What kind of detour—"

Another loud siren drowned him out. "It's so goddamn loud here," Victor huffed through the phone. "I need to go. Let's talk in a few days."

"Sure. Talk soon," said Oliver, hanging up.

"Can you translate?" she asked. Elbows were on the table as she leaned forward with folded arms.

"He only called to ask if I'd seen his credit card. Seems he lost it in Rome."

"What else?"

Oliver considered the conversation he'd had with Victor, everything said and unsaid. "It sounds like he's not going to be in Stockholm tomorrow as originally planned. Something about a detour."

"Did he say anything about coming here?" she pressed. "Or about where he's going?"

"It was really difficult to hear anything clearly," said Oliver.

Lucia lacked a self-consciousness of expression to hide her disappointment. Oliver felt he could understand everything about her if he didn't blink.

"He mentioned his meeting with the book buyer tomorrow,"

Oliver added. "I didn't get much else beyond that."

"Well, now he'll be using cash," said Lucia, letting out a deep sigh. "Which makes the ability to get any insight into his location near impossible." It was brief, but he saw hope cross her face. "Did he mention why he'd been here?"

"He didn't, but I know he's been meeting new clients for rare, collectible books," said Oliver. "He's been pretty dissatisfied with his job at a framer's shop for a while. Coming here could've been for a meeting with a new client."

"Or for a client wanting to buy the necklace," said Lucia bitterly.

"We don't know that for certain," said Oliver. He didn't know how to reassure her when he only had half the facts. He had no insight into the crime scene. The only information he knew was what Lucia told him. She shifted in her seat, her expression open and vulnerable. Victor's call had changed the tone of the quiet, intimate conversation they'd had before.

"I need to think, to plan, but I can hardly focus right now. I feel like we're so close to my mother's necklace."

And painfully far from it was left unsaid between them.

"Let's call it an evening and try to rest," suggested Oliver. "We can come up with a plan tomorrow."

"Oh?" Her eyes slid to his. "Is there now a 'we'?"

"I'm in this to help." Stubborn, wasn't she? "To fix it before it can't be undone. I will do everything I can to get your mother's necklace back to you. You have my word."

When a waiter came by to clear the table, she turned her attention to the wall of windows, nearby water unseen in the pall of night. He barely heard the clatter of china plates and voices around them. In the dimmed lighting of the restaurant, her eyes were a misty green, reminding him of a forest after a rainstorm.

CHAPTER EIGHTEEN

For the better part of an hour, Lucia tossed and turned. Sleep eluded her. Knots of restlessness and doubt were heavy anchors in the pit of her stomach.

After dinner with Oliver, she'd called Simon but had only been able to reach his voicemail. Her existence was in limbo, a disorienting in-between that greatly unsettled her. All she wanted was to keep propelling forward. With nothing to do but wait, she was overwhelmed with more questions. Nothing had happened according to plan since Rome.

Sighing into the dark of her hotel room, she relented to a walk to the ice machine. Lifting the hotel robe from a hook in the bathroom, she grabbed a peachy plastic bucket for ice.

Pocketing her room key in the robe, she made her way down the long, empty hallway. Frames of abstract art hung along the walls. A vending machine stood adjacent to the ice machine. A few scoops later, the bucket was full of ice chips in her arms. Bored, she deliberated the options of sugar and snacks. Faintly, she heard a *ding* of the elevator. Lamenting that she hadn't thought to bring her card or any cash, her eyes roamed over sweets on the fourth tier of the machine. Deciding to return with her card, Lucia made her way back down the long hallway. Her bare feet softly padded on the carpeted floor, ice making a soft rocking sound in her arms.

She stopped abruptly, turning to the elevator. Splayed apart, the doors opened to an empty carriage. She hadn't heard a door shut to any room nearby.

Don't be dramatic. She shook her head. Perhaps the break-in in Rome had made her paranoid. Someone probably exited the elevator while she was at the ice machine around the corner.

Doors lined each side of the hallway, with only a stairwell exit at one end and the vending and ice machines hidden out of view on the other. With a thudding heart, she felt a prickling sensation at the back of her neck.

The hallway, with its perfect golden wall lamps and patterned carpet, was vacant. Her hand slipped silently into the pocket where her room key was. *It's stupid; it's probably nothing but your imagination.* Her pupils dilated. Adrenaline coursed through her body as her hands shook. Air pushed into her, around her ears. She trembled as she inserted her room key.

A door closed loudly ahead of her, and she nearly jumped at the sight of a man and woman exiting the second elevator. With a confused expression at her reaction, their laughter was cut short. They continued past her and entered a room six doors down.

Lucia disappeared into her own room with relief. Leaning against the adjacent wall, she felt as if she'd free-dived a hundred meters and come up to the surface too quickly. Clutching the ice bucket, she peered into the small peephole. The fish-eye view it gave her was limited. She couldn't see anything except the quiet, unoccupied hallway.

***

The next morning, Lucia woke sharply from a light sleep before her alarm. Her eyes opened to the smooth white ceiling above her, and she pushed herself up to a sitting position. She'd lodged a chair beneath the handle of the door, and it was still at its odd angle. The chair was the only safety measure that let her sleep, eventually.

Everything felt different in daylight.

Cloaked in a cozy layer of darkness, the room was dim with the curtain drawn. Her feet made impressions on the rug as she went to the window. Pulling aside the thick fabric, a panoramic view of Amsterdam greeted her.

The slow movement of sunrise was a golden glow on gambrel roofs. A line of birds flew, stretched in an arc beneath scattered gray clouds. The start of day was a faint blue smudge in the sky. Below, she could see narrow rows of canals in the distance. Leaning on the sill, she surveyed bridges and rows of colonial-style homes. A few blocks north, she could see a pub with faded lettering. The canals were empty without the oblong, partially submerged boats in the water. Directly below, a van lumbered through the street in the direction of a bakery. Every sound was on mute from where she stood, but she could imagine them all. The rolling sound of tires over cobblestones woven with small weeds. Cyclists as they navigated the city with ease on two wheels.

She pulled a cashmere knit over her head and thought of Oliver a few doors down. It was very clear, now that she'd spent some time with him, that his work as a detective informed who he was. All indications pointed to a strong moral compass, but there was something deeper, too. He hadn't said anything overt, but she suspected he had lost someone. It was odd—the way death connected people. Grief could draw you to someone, collapsing all questions in exchange for understanding. *Me, too.* I know death and all it brings.

After a brief rinse of her face, she changed into warmer layers. The night before, she'd been able to secure an appointment at the US Consulate in Amsterdam for 8:30. Given the status of her missing passport, she was able to make an emergency appointment. Her research indicated she needed to bring a photocopy of her ID and her missing passport, as well as present some kind of itinerary for her travels. Staying in Amsterdam was contingent on updates to Victor's location, but her direct link to him was Oliver. Worse than the consequential countdown of finding Victor was the obligation to have a return flight booked. It was a requirement of the passport appointment, and it dragged forth all of Lucia's uncertainty like dregs in a swamp.

Taking a leap of decisiveness, she booked a one-way flight to New York from Stockholm. Her resolve, filled with conflicted hope and finality, was to still file a report against Victor in his home country. She couldn't let him get away with what he'd done, no matter the outcome.

Until that day, that flight, there was something she needed to see for herself in Amsterdam.

Lucia grabbed her hotel key card and placed basic essentials into her bag. Writing a quick note to Oliver on hotel stationery, she slipped it under his door. Once down on street level, her eyes absorbed the sight of everything that had appeared in miniature from her window. Everywhere were bicycles, rows and rows of them, rusted and new, chain-locked to metal stands. Glancing at her phone, she had a general sense of direction and began walking. Slipping her phone, room key, and cash into her leather pouch, she was glad her wallet had been kept separately inside her bag at the time her room had been robbed.

At the sight of a cab turning a nearby street corner, she waved a hand to catch his attention.

Though the day before had brought a chilly breeze, the morning already seemed to have a warmer start. The ride to the US consulate was brief, less than fifteen minutes door to door. But in those minutes, she watched unfamiliar streets of the city pass by. Block after block were tall and narrow brick-layered homes. Lace curtains hung in windows, with an array of trinkets on sills. Cats eyed pedestrians on sidewalks. A man in a paperboy hat and tweed jacket sat alone around the corner from a cafe, reading a newspaper. Streets were filled with bicycles stacked against one another. In front of the consulate, Lucia paid the cab driver. After making her way through the security entrance, she meticulously filled out the required forms and provided all the documentation needed. The process itself wasn't long since she'd been able to print copies of her birth certificate and New York ID at the hotel. The passport agent, a woman in her fifties with wispy blonde hair, accepted her documents, including Lucia's return flight details and flight number. She assured the agent a fraud alert had already been placed to prevent identity theft.

"Do you want to file a police report?"

"I made sure to file a police report already," Lucia answered in half-truth. The agent processed the paperwork and took her photo. With a firm smile and a nod, Lucia was out the door in under three hours with a temporary emergency passport. Outside the consulate, she made her way in the direction of the canals. Given her early start, it wasn't quite noon yet.

With a destination and ticket on her phone, she walked past parks and homes and restaurants, the city bustling with the good weather. As she made her way toward the Oud-West district, she wondered if she was walking down the same streets her mother had during any of her visits throughout the years. Was she surprised that she'd never visited the city with her mother? Perhaps there was less to be surprised by when she really considered how infrequently they ever saw each other despite living in Manhattan, long before becoming estranged. Putting one foot in front of the other, tension bloomed in her chest. Cherry blossoms swept through the air like snow. Lucia walked by wagons filled with greenery. With a quick stop in a cafe, she ordered a coffee. While she waited, she stood by an arch of the front window. Her mother never enjoyed sweets and often touted her belief that giving into one's cravings implied weakness. Except on Lucia's birthdays. Buried in a vague memory, Lucia could hear her mother's voice saying, *a sweet for little Starling darling.* The only nickname her mother had ever given her. One of the rare, forgotten endearments of kindness, which, too, held a sort of grief to untangle.

A barista handed Lucia her takeaway coffee, which she accepted greedily. Pushing through the door, she continued onward. Lucia walked until the house came into view. She paused, transfixed at a street corner. There it was: the Anne Frank house.

A place that had gripped her mother. The Holocaust and everything Jewish families had lost in the war moved Rowan in a way Lucia had never really seen before. Over the years, Lucia had witnessed her mother hand-deliver lost artifacts to families in New York and beyond. Her mother's ability to recover stolen heirlooms that had been lost helped mend wounds born from a terrible war. Rowan's dedication to doing so made her a hero to many people, but Lucia was torn between the woman people knew and the mother she'd had. It was harder to be angry with an exemplar.

Now, standing before the house, years of resentment and anger slipped through her fingers. Lucia accepted that her mother's emotional unavailability had never been about her. For the first time, she could divorce herself from the insult of her mother's absence. Maybe Rowan had been right to once say that correcting history was bigger than anything else. Would that mean Lucia was obligated to forgive her? If she absolved her for this, would the whole of her distress topple with it?

Eyes brimming, Lucia's mercurial nostalgia swirled in the morning light. She thought of Rowan's stories of Amsterdam and her nickname and the years they lost and the funeral and the necklace. Memories of her mother had become the eye of a hurricane in her sorrow. It hadn't mattered that she'd left New York. Resentment and love had both survived despite Rowan's death, following her here to Amsterdam. She'd clung to the potential of her mother and had never fully reconciled the tension in their relationship. The swirl of emotions brought to mind a word she'd read somewhere years before.

Hiraeth.

She'd never forgotten its meaning; she was indeed homesick for a place she could never go.

Lucia went to the entrance to present her ticket. Stepping through the doors, Lucia took it all in. Here was where Anne Frank had made her way up a narrow set of steps eighty years before and her mother less than a decade ago. It ached to bring herself to the same place Rowan had once been—as if time had been carried across entire oceans and continents, shepherding Lucia back to the mother who had once been her homeland.

CHAPTER NINETEEN

Oliver woke the next morning, a sliver of light coming in through a gap in the curtains.

Sitting up, he placed his feet to rest on the frame of the bed and rubbed the sleep from his eyes. His fingertips pressed into his right temple. He thought of Lucia.

She surprised him.

He suspected that beyond the strained circumstances of how they met, she was an intense and deeply feeling person. That something inconsolable beneath the surface motivated her. Attempting to travel to Sweden by herself was definitely bold, but his assessment was that it hadn't been impulsivity guiding her but determination. Control for recourse, perhaps.

That her relationship with her mother had been challenging only confirmed it. Family relationships could be tricky, as he knew well.

His feet padded against the velvet rug as he walked past the credenza to the bathroom.

On the floor near the door lay a note from Lucia, her handwriting scrawled across hotel stationery with wide looped l's.

> *Oliver,*
>
> *Need to take care of something. Meet me at Cafe Brecht? 4 o'clock.*
>
> *— Lucia*

Oliver grabbed his toothbrush and put a splash of water on the bristles. While he brushed his teeth, he considered her multifaceted contradictions. He would hardly ever describe himself as someone who struggled with indecision, yet there he was, labored with it since meeting Lucia on the train.

Disjointed in his thoughts of her were thoughts of Victor. If his cousin really did steal her mother's necklace—evidence was surely piling against him—it complicated everything. The effects would ripple through his family boundlessly: trust broken and Victor's mother left on her own again, without a husband or a son.

There was still a large gap between what he knew and what he didn't. Lucia claimed she'd found Victor's train ticket. The fact that the receipts had Victor's name and card information made it impossible to deny. Victor was known for being brash, but he'd never heard his cousin talk about jewelry or luxury items. In the years since being released from jail, Victor's behavior seemed different.

Had he simply become better at hiding his true impulses? Something didn't sit right with Oliver. At work, he could compartmentalize cases; it was muscle memory. But life was messier.

Perhaps he was easier to manipulate because he cared for Victor. It was hard to deny that family members of a criminal had blind spots. He had seen the duality of Victor: his impatience spurred on by his temper, and his generosity. In Oliver's work, interviewing witnesses related to the suspect and getting character testimony went a long way in understanding motive. Did he get so wrapped up in believing Victor could change, that he *had* changed, that he'd missed what was right in front of him?

For now, he was willing to follow Lucia's lead. So far, her information about Victor had been correct. Even the part about him being in Amsterdam, which Oliver hadn't even known. He wondered about her source of information. Oliver ran hot water in the shower. The best course of action might be to confront Victor in Sweden. It could be the most resolute avenue forward to stop him from hiding anything else. Not his reaction, the necklace, or the truth.

***

Around 16:15, Oliver saw Lucia make her way across the street in his direction. He was caught off guard by the sight of her.

She spotted him and waved. Nothing about her or being around her felt casual. It would be dishonest to deny his attraction for her, but he tried to set it aside.

"From what I hear about Amsterdam, this is probably one of four days in the year when it's sunny," said Lucia by way of greeting. Stepping onto the patio, she pulled out a cafe chair to sit across from him.

"I wonder what they do with the other three days."

She settled into her seat and grabbed a menu. A feeling grew between his shoulder blades to reach toward her. Instead, he folded his hands in his lap. She opened the menu. He watched her read down the wine list.

"I had the oddest sensation of being followed last night."

"What do you mean?" asked Oliver.

"I couldn't sleep, so I went to the ice machine around midnight. As I walked back, the elevator doors were open, except no one was there." She pushed strands of hair out of her face. "It's probably nothing."

"But it didn't feel like that," stated Oliver.

"It felt like someone was nearby." Suspicion flickered across her face. "Like I was being watched."

"I believe you. I actually had the same feeling."

"What, you mean here?" Lucia peered at him above her menu, glancing around them.

"When I was in Rome with Victor," said Oliver. "Nothing obvious, but it was a feeling. What do you call that in English?"

"Intuition."

"Hm."

"If we're being followed, could it be connected to Victor?" she asked with concern. "Do you think he knows we're onto him?"

"A feeling isn't proof. We'd need more than that."

"You are annoyingly thorough."

They sat in silence, listening to the busy street. Cyclists and mopeds zoomed by. Life was in the canals, families shopping at markets under a cloudless sky. He watched her take a sip of water from the glass that was beginning to sweat on the square table.

"I'd like to tell you about Victor's father."

"What does his father have to do with anything?" asked Lucia with narrowed eyes.

"When we were fifteen, Victor's father, my uncle, was murdered. I was there when the officers delivered the news." He gently placed his palm on the table and leaned forward to meet her eyes. He was close enough to see the irises, the orb of focus. He could see the edge of wariness, too.

"What happened?"

"He was having an affair." A flash of his aunt collapsing rang in his memory. "The husband of the woman found out. It ended ... violently."

Lucia's hands folded beneath her chin, studying him. "Your uncle's death is why you became a detective, isn't it?"

His mouth parted in surprise. Somehow, she'd cut through all that had been left unsaid. "Yes."

"It's not that I don't have sympathy, but I wasn't particularly close with my mother. You don't see me going around robbing people."

"I'm not here to defend him." Oliver shook his head. "I'm in no way excusing what he's done. I'm of the belief that with anything in life, context can be useful."

"I guess," she nodded. "So your uncle died, and you became someone who solves crimes, while Victor became someone who commits them."

"It's important to understand it wasn't *my* father," said Oliver, running his hand through his hair in frustration with himself. He wasn't explaining it correctly. "He was typically indifferent to Victor, but it was worse when he was cruel. There was a lot of tension between them. But Victor has never been the same since the murder. Our family hasn't been the same."

"I'm not a sociopath," said Lucia with a relenting sigh. Her expression softened. "I do feel terrible for you and your family. It sounds horrible."

"After my uncle's murder, I became obsessed about the case. I poured over publicly available reports and news articles. I approached one of the officers who had told us the news that day. He withheld forensics, but he let me read the reports about the man who killed my uncle and the woman he'd had an affair with. Apparently, the husband had a history of violence. After graduation, I enrolled in training to become an officer, and eventually, I became a sergeant."

"You wanted what you do to matter to families who need closure," said Lucia gently. At Oliver's affirmation, she asked, "What does your family think about your job?"

"My younger sister Tuva says it suits me well. Linnea ... I'm not actually sure. I've never asked. As the oldest, she has a different perspective of the entire thing."

"How many siblings do you have?"

"Two, though I'll only admit to one if they're both around," said Oliver with a small lift of his mouth.

"What does Linnea do?"

"She's a medical researcher. She conducts clinical trials for new treatments specific to fatal diseases. She's currently doing one for cardiac sarcoma, which affects the—"

"—pericardium around the heart," interrupted Lucia.

"That's impressive," said Oliver. "Do you usually memorize random medical conditions?"

"I don't. It's only because my—" Lucia cut off. All of a sudden gripping the table, her attention was fixated behind him.

"No *fucking* way."

CHAPTER TWENTY

It was the color of the dress, a familiar pastel, that drew her gaze. Lucia hadn't seen it since she'd placed it on the bed next to the necklace. A stunning and lithe redhead wearing the dress was about to pass them on the sidewalk. Lucia knew without a doubt it was her dress. She'd purchased it on a trip to San Francisco in a thrift store two years before.

"No *fucking* way."

Oliver turned in the direction she was staring. Pushing back in her chair, Lucia strode toward the woman. Less than ten feet away, Lucia stopped herself. Was there a chance she could be wrong? Was she about to accost a perfectly innocent person? Before she could take another step forward, Oliver went up to the woman, blocking her.

"I know you," said Oliver.

Lucia whipped her attention to Oliver.

The woman seemed entirely confused, glancing around the patio where a few people were ogling.

"Excuse me? You are ... ?"

"We've met. I was with my cousin in Rome. Victor?"

Her ears were ringing as a million questions raced through her mind. She moved to stand beside him as a group of men in suits tried to get by. She pointed to a small bench across the street. "Why don't we take this conversation over there?"

The woman shrugged, leading the way. In a small triangle of grass stood a black lamppost, flowers growing over the base. At the bench, she pulled out a lighter and cigarette. She clicked the metal cap shut at the inhale. Crossing her legs, she arched a brow, waiting.

"That is my dress," said Lucia coldly. "Why are you wearing it?"

"I didn't realize someone could be interrogated over their fashion choices," said the woman as she inhaled gently, blowing smoke over her shoulder.

"My dress, the one you're wearing, went missing the same night as my necklace. I got it at a thrift store, which makes it highly unusual that it's in your possession."

Wearing an unreadable expression, the woman stared at her. After a moment, she pointed to Lucia with the same fingers holding her cigarette.

"You."

"Yes? What about me?" demanded Lucia.

"I remember you now." The woman said to Oliver, speaking with an accent Lucia couldn't quite place. "Victor and I spent two days in Rome together after we met. He had to pick up some book but said he would meet me after. We were having lunch near a hotel that you," an elegant finger pointed to Lucia, "were walking into. He had just met you—some catastrophe or another—and he was quite upset about the book. I left to meet my friend shortly after that."

"That explains how he found out where you were staying," said Oliver to Lucia, crossing his arms.

"So he recognized me, then followed me in." Lucia turned to the redhead. "That doesn't explain my dress."

"How embarrassing, as I thought it was a gift," said the woman. She took another long drag, her lipstick staining the white filter. "Would you like it back right now? I don't mind."

Lucia scowled.

"Tough crowd," said the woman with a sigh. "After lunch, Victor packed up, and he met me at Schiphol airport. I received this dress as a gift."

"Did he also give you my passport he stole?" asked Lucia. She ignored the surprised expression on Oliver's face.

"What on earth would I do with your passport when I have my own?"

The woman took another drag of her cigarette. "All I can tell you is that we flew together to Amsterdam. He left yesterday for Berlin."

In bewilderment, Lucia could see it all in her mind's eye as it had happened. Victor had seen her walking into her hotel in Rome, decided to follow her to her hotel room, and found a way in. He might've even walked through the entrance and was presumed to be a guest. Stealing the necklace would make him money, but taking her passport and dress was personal. The fact that he'd taken all three infuriated her.

"Is he coming back?" asked Oliver.

"He's your cousin; don't you know?"

"Let's assume I do, but why don't you tell us," said Lucia.

"He left for Berlin yesterday evening to meet the buyer of the book," said the woman, flicking off ash, "He's returning tomorrow after meeting a last-minute client."

Lucia's stomach dropped to the cold concrete. "For another book?

"No," said the woman. "For some kind of jewelry item."

Lucia turned to Oliver. "Everything she's saying lines up with what we know. He had a flight out of Schiphol by the time we got off the train." It was startling to realize she'd been in Amsterdam for only a day. It felt like a week. "Are you thinking what I'm thinking?"

"If we leave tonight, we can be in Berlin," said Oliver. He turned to the woman. "Did he give you an address?"

"Can't you just call him yourself?" The woman asked, puzzled.

"It's complicated," interrupted Lucia. "The situation is a bit fluid right now, and your help would really mean a lot."

"Sure," said the woman, waving a dismissive hand in the air. "I only met this guy a few days ago. I didn't know he was in so much trouble."

"Can we contact you in case he reaches out?" asked Oliver.

The woman's red hair swished in movement as she opened up her handbag of thin leather with a silver chain, no larger than an oversized envelope.

"This is my business card." She handed it to Lucia. "I own one of the dispensaries in the city."

Lucia read the name of the business and the address, nodding. She handed the card to Oliver.

"I know this was abrupt, but thank you for talking with us," said Lucia. She gestured toward the cafe. Oliver nodded.

"Happy to help," said the woman.

"What's your—" Her words stuck in her throat. A song on a speaker played somewhere nearby. The door to a nearby shop had opened, and she could hear the beginning of a Fleetwood Mac song. Lucia partially turned around, trying to locate where the sound was coming from.

"Lucia? Were you saying something?" Oliver placed a hand on her arm.

Lucia could hear the chorus, could remember the last time she'd heard the song all those years before, burrowed in a dark memory of her mother. With a fast-beating heart, she turned toward the woman. "I was going to say, I didn't see your name on the card. What's your name?"

"Mia," said the redhead, standing up. She crushed her cigarette beneath the wedge of her right shoe. "My name is Mia."

Chapter Twenty-One

The brisk air fogged in front of Lucia as she and her boyfriend, Jiro, walked up the steps of her parent's two-story brownstone. She was committed to getting through Christmas dinner unscathed. Well, as least-scathed as possible.

"What's your mom's name again?" asked Jiro. Lucia's hand had been poised to knock. His raven-black hair shone from the porch light above them.

"Rowan, remember?" said Lucia, lowering her hand. "And my dad's name is Daniel."

"Maybe we should've had me meet them on a different day." Jiro fidgeted, chewing on his lip.

"You waited to voice objections until now?" She shifted the pie in her hand against her chest. "Really?"

"There's just so much pressure on a holiday. Hey, don't be mad," said Jiro, reaching his ungloved hand to her shoulder.

"We've been dating for nearly a year and have talked about moving in together. It feels like an important step."

"I mean, things have been going so well ... " Jiro drifted off. "I'm just saying. You're the one who told me you have a tense relationship. It doesn't exactly make me thrilled to be here."

Lucia's frustrations mounted below the surface. For much of her dating life, she'd avoided a meet-the-parents milestone for this exact reason. She didn't want the strain or the emotional exposure. The idea of bringing a boyfriend to witness the tension first-hand was a knot inside her stomach. Family seemed vastly different to her friends, whose warm stories of interactions always held a fictitious quality against her experience. She'd always felt like an outsider who could peer into the lives of her friends, but she herself would never inhabit their world. Much to the encouragement of Simon, he'd suggested she try it first before admitting defeat. After six months of therapy, she was willing to try doing things differently. Yet, her stomach was tight with anxiety and a wild imagination of all the ways it could go wrong.

"We're already here. Let's just get this over with," muttered Lucia. Her cold fist gave two quick rasps against the front door.

The warm air from inside was a slow drift to the porch when her father answered. "Merry Christmas, everyone," he said with a smile. His arm opened wide to welcome them in. "Your mother is in the kitchen finishing the gravy."

"This is Jiro," said Lucia as she shrugged off her jacket to hang it on the rack near the door. "Jiro, this is my father."

"Nice to meet you, sir," said Jiro. He stuck out his hand.

"Please, call me Daniel. I was fixing a drink just now. Would you like one?" Her father motioned to the bar cart. Jiro's eyes widened slightly in admiration at the gold-lined cart with shelves full of bottles of gin, bourbon, and mixers. Losing her boyfriend to the art of a cocktail, her eyes floated in the direction of the kitchen.

"I'll help Mom, I guess," she said. The two of them were oblivious, talking about a brand of scotch her father was pouring into a glass.

"Sounds good," replied Jiro without turning.

Why the hell are women still relegated to the kitchen in the twenty-first century?

Turning on her heel, she made her way down the long hallway toward the kitchen. The dining table was set with four china plates, utensils and glassware in a geometric shape with chinaware at the center. Making her way into the entry of the kitchen, she set her phone down on the credenza in case she needed to carry plates out. Lucia held back a sigh before letting it loose. She fixed a smile on her face.

"Hi, Mom," said Lucia as she pushed open the kitchen door.

"Oh, good," said Rowan without turning. "You can help me carry dishes into the dining room." Her mother's tan hands worked fast, scooping food onto serving platters.

"Sure," replied Lucia. She reached for two of the platters, but a serving fork of one clattered to the ground.

"Be careful!" Her mother finally turned. Bending to pick up the fork, the necklace peeked out, dangling mid-air before disappearing again as Rowan placed the utensil in the sink. She grabbed another from a nearby drawer. "Try not to drop this one."

"I've been here twenty seconds; could you just chill?" said Lucia. "I want you to meet Jiro."

Her mother raised her eyebrows. "Who is Jiro?"

"My boyfriend."

"I thought you were dating Lucas?"

"I only dated him for, like, three months," Lucia scoffed before she could stop herself. "*Two* years ago."

"You can't expect me to keep up."

Lucia gripped the handles of the dish in her hands. *Don't start a fight on Christmas.*

"There's not been many, and just one right now."

"Don't let the food get cold." Her mom indicated with her chin in the direction of the dining room. "I'll finish the gravy and meet Jiro."

Lucia brought out the platters and gently placed them on the table. Regardless of how they got along, she couldn't deny her mother had exquisite taste as a hostess. After a round of introductions, they sat for dinner. Lucia took a long sip from a drink her father had poured her. Ice rattled in the cup as her parents shared a story about a recent trip to Greece, the colorful lights of the Christmas tree filling the front window. Lucia wondered about the view from the outside. If anyone peered in, would they only see the china plates, her mother's chic bun, the expensive scotch?

"Thank you for hosting," said Jiro and turned to Rowan, pleased with himself. "You're not as bad as Lucia said you'd be."

Fantastic.

"I wouldn't believe everything she says," said Rowan with a tight smile. She took a sip of her wine.

"Who wants another drink? Jiro?"

The tight leash of her exasperation was slipping. "I don't want—" Lucia began.

"Have a drink." Her mother waved a hand. "It'll help you relax for the holiday."

"Do you have any more scotch?" Jiro asked. Lucia tried to kick his chair leg under the table. He ignored it.

"Only the best. Do you like Signet?"

Jiro drifted back to the bar with her father. Lucia felt invisible again. As if all the feelings swirling inside of her weren't real to anyone else. She'd felt unseen for so long that bringing Jiro to meet her parents had the opposite outcome of what she'd wanted. She wanted them to behave differently, to be different, but how foolish it was when she really thought about it. She'd wanted something more, and instead, all she had was what they gave.

"How is work?" asked Rowan, ever an expert at small talk, between neat bites.

"Fine," said Lucia blandly. At this rate, if she kept biting her tongue, she'd bleed.

"Not everything has to be difficult, you know," her mother commented.

"I really enjoy working at the UN." Lucia relaxed her jaw and gave a poor attempt at a smile. "Right now, it's mostly administrative tasks. I'm gathering data from disparate sources so that my team can compile a master document for an upcoming conference. I like my boss."

"That's good."

Lucia's gaze wandered over to the bar where her father and Jiro stood. She could overhear them discussing the merits of various whiskeys. Tired, she set her fork down.

"That's it?"

"Is what it?" Rowan took another bite.

"It's just … you ask me a question about work. I share information about my life, and you offer nothing else. You never ask follow-up questions," said Lucia, her voice growing louder. "I don't understand why every conversation has to be surface level."

"You're being quite hostile today," said her mother, surprised.

"I can't—I can't be here anymore," Queasy, Lucia pushed out her chair and stood. "Ask me how I feel about something, *anything*, and that can be a conversation. Otherwise, I'd rather just be at home."

"Lucia," said her father, a tone of warning. Jiro shifted, appearing uncomfortable.

Lucia hadn't known her threshold for suffering until now. Her father across the room, her mother to her right. Lucia in the middle, always between a feeling and a fact. Stark clarity rang like a bell. "I'm not difficult. I'm not asking for too much. I am not a task to check off your to-do list and then be forgotten."

"What do you want from me?" asked Rowan in a low voice. Lucia knew that voice. It was the *don't make a scene* tone.

"I want you to be a mother!" shouted Lucia. Arguments with

Rowan were a grave she'd repeatedly dug herself into over the years. Would she never learn? "I just want you to care," said Lucia. "Is that too much to ask?"

"Yes, goddammit, Lucia," her mother's fork clattered unceremoniously on the plate. Each of them was like a wolf, jaws snapping in retaliation against each other. "It is. Okay? Are you happy now? You are *too* much, *too* difficult. I hardly ever know what to do with you. We don't need to always discuss every feeling or thought that passes through you. Some things can just be, and it's *fine*." Rowan's last sentence was emphasized with a snarl, a scowl, a set of eyes dark as the night.

Lucia walked towards the coat rack and began to put her jacket on. "We're leaving, Jiro."

"Ah, I—um, thank you, sir. I suppose we're going." Jiro fumbled, handing her father his glass. Her father gave Lucia a look of concern. She ignored it as Jiro grabbed his own coat.

"It was nice to—meet you both." Jiro cleared his throat, and they walked out the door.

Lucia was anything but calm as she descended the steps. Rage held her captive, but even deeper than that was profound sadness. It threaded her skin together, keeping her from falling apart. Who was she, if not the person her mother said she was?

"Couldn't you have just kept it polite?" asked Jiro while they walked down the block. Jiro's hands were in his pockets as they walked. "It would have been nice to at least get through dinner."

"In case you missed it," said Lucia, spinning in his direction, "the entire exchange had nothing to do with you. It would have been comforting if you had been there as an ally. Instead, you were there to drink my father's expensive scotch."

"Hey—" His palms faced her mid-air. Frosted air floated between them like a cloud. "I'm not the enemy. You seem as much of the problem as you make them out to be."

Lucia's bitterness rose to the surface and came out as a dangerous whisper. "I'm done, Jiro."

"Done?" He stopped walking. "We're breaking up? You're breaking up with me?"

"I'm only doing what you would have done eventually," said Lucia. Her resolve landed with the snow as it fell to the ground around them.

"I can't believe this—on Christmas!"

"There would never have been a good time," Lucia pointed out. "You don't seem ready for a relationship anyway."

"You're a real bitch," he said. "I should've never asked you to move in with me."

She took a silent, imperceptible step towards him. Jiro took a half-step back.

"Get the fuck out of here, Jiro. Or I'll prove to you just how much of a bitch I really can be."

Jiro's rapid exhales met more snow, which began to fall in earnest.

"Don't call me," said Lucia with steeled resolve. "Don't text. Don't show up with coffee next week with apologies. I'm done."

He shook his head, shoving his hands into his pocket. Turning, he walked away and out of her life. She only felt relief. Snow clung to the tendrils of her hair. Raising her palm, she watched it melt on her skin. When she reached for her phone, her coat pockets were empty. Narrowing her eyes, she rummaged through her handbag.

"Motherfucker." She cursed to the sky as it emptied above her, turning the city into a landscape of white.

Turning on her heel, she took the path to her parents' home. At their door, she peered in through the windows beyond the tree. The table was a still life of half-empty wine glasses and disheveled napkins. She spotted her phone on top of the credenza, where she'd left it. Quietly inching the door open, she paused where the cold met warm air. She only wanted to get her phone and go. A low murmur of her parents talking could be heard from the kitchen. Her father's Bluetooth speaker was softly playing Fleetwood Mac. Her mother's voice carried through.

"... Honestly, I don't know why she acts that way. It's exhausting."

Lucia crept toward the credenza, which stood just outside the door to the kitchen. The swinging door was closed, with a half-inch gap only showing a sliver of a sweater and her mother's hair. Lucia sidestepped a spot in the floorboard that might creak and give her away. Dishes clattered in the sink.

"Try to love her the way she's asking for," said her father over the sound of running water. "I know your career is very important to you, but try to remember you're also a mother."

"I don't *want* to be remembered as a mother. I want to be remembered for my legacy, and that's bigger than her."

Lucia halted. Stevie Nicks crooned, singing about love and lies and shadows.

"Don't say that, Rowan." She could hear her father's voice now. Almost pleading. "I know you both get so mad sometimes, but I think it's only because you both care so much."

"So you're taking her side?" Her mother's voice was fractured with agitation.

"No—now, Rowan, don't get upset—"

"I have sacrificed so much of myself for this family." Her mother's tinny voice rose above the clatter of glassware clinking. "What do I get in return? Ingratitude. Hostility. You're the one who wanted children, Dan. I never wanted to be a mother."

The kick drum of the song beat in the spaces where Lucia's own heart had stopped.

"You don't mean that," said her father with hurt in his voice. "Could you imagine if she heard you say such a thing?"

Lucia gripped her phone in her hand and began to walk backward in silent motion. Her hip jostled a chair, which she tried to steady before it made a scratching noise across the floor.

"I'm going to grab the platter we left out," said her mother a split second before pushing through the door of the kitchen. Rowan's hands were full of soap and water. The door swung shut behind her.

Eternity stood between them in surprise, in guilt, in regret. Within the silence of the dining room, Lucia startled at her father's voice calling from the kitchen. "Do you need help grabbing it?"

Her mother didn't answer him, instead watching Lucia carefully.

With one last, long look, Lucia turned to make her way to the front door. She shut it quietly behind her as she put her parents' home at her back. She wanted to carve a slice of the earth and bury herself in it, where it was dark and quiet.

She had always believed her mother felt that way, so she wasn't sure why it still surprised her to hear Rowan admit it. Lucia had always wondered if the darkness inside her heart was so vast it put anyone in peril who might dare to try and love her. She didn't *feel* danger, she realized. *She* was the danger. And anyone she might come into contact with would fall in and lose their way. Her mother's words felt as if they'd given her a new identity. With those seven words, *I never wanted to be a mother,* she felt desolate. There was no satisfaction in seeing her mother realize Lucia had heard everything.

Manhattan was a haze of lights in her periphery, and snow underfoot muted her steps as she made the long walk home. She barely felt the cold. Sidewalks were empty as if everyone was celebrating while she mourned. New York City was a glimmer of holiday spirit at the edge of rooftops and darkened restaurants and cherry trees bare of their color and trash cans filled to the brim and homes full of warmth and cheer. For her, on lonely streets home, there was only silence, steep with what would come next.

Chapter Twenty-Two

By the time they'd returned to the hotel, a plan was in motion. Hastily, Lucia packed while Oliver was in his room doing the same. She anticipated her father could help with two last-minute plane tickets to Berlin. Although she'd seen a tense look cross Oliver's face at the mention of a flight, he'd only nodded in agreement with the plan to go to Berlin and confront Victor in person. She dialed her father's number, putting in both wireless earbuds for the call, as she went through every drawer to ensure nothing was left behind.

"Lucia." His greeting was mixed with surprise and relief, pressing into her guilt like pressure on a fresh wound.

"Dad." She hesitated. "I'm really sorry I haven't called until now."

"Uh oh. It sounds like there's a 'but,'" said Daniel. A suitcase rolling on its wheels could be heard on the other end.

"There is. I ... need your help."

"What's wrong?" he asked with concern. "Are you hurt?"

"I'm safe," she reassured him. "But I need your help getting to Berlin."

"I thought you were staying in Italy," he said. "But you need a flight to Germany?"

"I was—in Rome," said Lucia haltingly. Thoughts and explanations rapidly overlapped, briefly paralyzing her. Where would she even begin? "There's not much time to explain—it's really, terribly important. Would you be able to secure two flights out of Amsterdam to Berlin for tonight?"

"You gotta give me twenty minutes to call Lewis," said Daniel. His voice was subdued, but he offered his help. "It'll likely be standby seats, but I'll make it happen."

As the Director of Aviation Security at Heathrow, Lewis was an old family friend from her father's pilot school day. She breathed a sigh of relief.

"Thank you," said Lucia. She could hear the sound of a car door shutting. "Where are you right now?"

"I'm working a few days in Vancouver."

"So soon?"

"I think it's best to be around people right now," said her father with measured words. She imagined him in his uniform, the view out the window of another city. "Being without your mom has been hard."

Lucia stopped folding her sweater and sat on the corner of the bed. Staring at the blank screen of the TV, her silhouette was a dark reflection. She'd been so upset after the will reading, so wrapped up in her own anguish, that she'd barely considered his. Guilt hung heavy in her arms, another thing to carry in this life. "Would you like to talk once we're both back home?" she asked.

"I would." A pause. "I know I haven't always done my best, but I'm here for you," he said ruefully. As if it was the easiest thing to say in the world. "Always."

Emotion bobbed in her throat, and she stared at the sweater in her hands, unsure of what to say.

"I do need to call Lewis now if you need those tickets for tonight," he said.

"Yes, right." She cleared her throat. "I'll text you the two passport numbers for the tickets."

After hanging up, Lucia removed her earbuds and placed them in her bag. As she began closing her suitcase, she caught sight of the envelope sticking halfway out of an inside pocket. Her nickname written in the curved slope of her mother's handwriting. Why had she brought it to Rome in the first place? For closure, maybe. Or maybe it was time to admit the letter was a piece of the puzzle that made Rowan best left unsolved.

Above Amsterdam, a sky full of evening clouds stood watch over the city, threatening rain. Scanning the room a final time, her hands briefly raised to her neck. She closed her fist, then eased it open to grab the handle of her luggage. In the hallway, Oliver stood waiting, and she shut the door quietly without a backward glance.

CHAPTER TWENTY-THREE

Samaran monitored the entrance of a well-lit hotel from across the street. Thunder rumbled as he sheltered beneath an awning of a small cafe. It gave him an advantageous standpoint to see who came in and out. He smoked to kill time. In the past twenty four hours, he'd made slow progress in Amsterdam, much to his regret. The Swede he'd tracked from Rome had been far more difficult to follow than anticipated.

In his nineteen years of investigative work, he had become accustomed to the sprint and waning nature of its pace. He'd spent a decade as an officer in Coventry before taking on private clients. A referral from a previous job had connected him to his current client, an owner of a renowned gallery in Copenhagen who had been robbed of an emerald and two other rare art items. The history behind the pieces was a bit esoteric for his taste, but he liked a client who paid well. With stolen goods valued at over 495 thousand euros, he'd been promised nine percent of the amount from the pieces he could recover.

He couldn't afford to refuse the opportunity. Yet, somehow, six days later, he wasn't any closer to finding what'd been stolen from his client.

After the nightclub in Rome, he'd done some reconnaissance to dig up a name, any name. *Something.* His inquiry with hotel staff had yielded few results. Unless it was an official investigation conducted by local police, staff were fairly reticent to share confidential guest information. Providing his identification made a modicum of progress, getting him one piece of information: a single name. With it, he'd placed a trace on the Swede's card after cross-referencing his initial mode of travel—the train was an odd, inefficient choice, but what did he care—which brought Samaran to Amsterdam. After a quick review of his background, he was even more confused about the Swede. Samaran didn't understand what a detective would want with jewels and heirlooms.

He mulled over his next move. Should he take a firm approach? Reaching into his coat pocket, he slipped his hand into the inner left pocket to check the safety of his gun.

Unexpectedly, the man he'd been following rushed out of the hotel with a dark-haired woman. Together, they ducked into a taxi, fleeing sight. He'd nearly missed them through the downpour.

Wait a damn minute. Samaran took a step toward the curb, the flame of his cigarette extinguished by rain. *What happened to the redhead?*

Chapter Twenty-Four

At the airport, Lucia and Oliver checked in at the counter for tickets held under each of their names. Lewis had forwarded the ticket information for a flight departing in less than two hours. Grateful, she guessed he'd really pulled some strings to move that fast—and made a mental note to send him an expensive bottle of cognac, his favorite, in thanks. The conversation she'd have with her father once she returned to New York was even more important but far trickier than nice liquor.

As they moved through a metal detector, each dutifully removed electronics and toiletries from their luggage. Being at the airport with Oliver made for an oddly intimate experience.

Rows of screens displayed arrivals, delays, and departures. Patrons scrolled on their phones in designated dining areas. Rolling wheels of suitcases passed, their small tags waving by a string. Having a father who was a pilot made the habits and scenes of the airport a familiar comfort. Perfume bottles and duty-free lotions sat neatly on acrylic shelves, beckoning foreigners and bourgeois women in silk scarves. Time was a whirlpool in an airport, where drinking at nine in the morning and sleeping across rows of chairs seemed fairly acceptable.

In the span of a week, she'd been in planes, trains, and taxis. New York City seemed an alternate universe, a place where a different version of her lived that didn't resemble all she'd been through since she'd left. Nothing would be the same until she could find her mother's necklace.

After making it through security, Lucia checked her ticket and then a monitor.

"We're at gate twenty seven. It's the next terminal over," said Lucia. Gesturing to the gate number above them with the number twelve, he nodded. She felt his gaze as they walked.

"Yes?"

"I'm guessing you didn't have a passport when you left Rome."

A brief hum of neutrality escaped her lips.

"And," continued Oliver, "you have a passport now. Otherwise, we wouldn't be able to board this flight. Is this why you were taking a train?"

"Let's say hypothetically—not as an admission of guilt—" she shot him a look, "that I didn't have my passport while traveling between countries. It's important to recognize that US consulates in most European countries take emergency appointments to issue replacements on the same day, should you need them. Ah, hypothetically."

"Mmhm," said Oliver. His eyes flitted to her luggage.

She followed his attention. "You're suddenly very chatty," said

Lucia.

"You pack very minimally, considering how long you had planned to travel," Oliver observed. Their pace was quick as they traversed across the terminal's clean, white tiles.

"You mean I pack light for a *woman*," accused Lucia.

"With a mother and two sisters, I value my life too much to assume that kind of stereotype about you," said Oliver.

"It's admirable that you've kept your sense of humor despite your fear of flying."

He let out a surprised laugh. "Here, I thought *I* was the behavior expert."

"Your life flashing before your eyes when I mentioned 'plane' was a dead giveaway."

A flight number and gate change announcement came over the speaker, nearly drowning out a voice calling out behind them. Oliver turned first, and she followed his stare. A man jogged in their direction, a leather backpack in his hand. Out of breath, he grasped Oliver's shoulder with a friendly smile. Frozen in place, Lucia's eyes grew wide as Victor huffed and set his bag on the ground.

"Didn't you hear me calling your name?"

CHAPTER TWENTY-FIVE

ROME

Officer Costa stepped into the lobby of the *Fontana Blu* hotel, its entryway flanked by two velvet chairs. Making his way to the marble counters, two clerks stood organizing sightseeing brochures. He was struck by a sense of déjà vu from when he'd first come to write the report of the theft.

Intrigued by Ivan's reports of other related thefts, Costa had extensively reviewed his notes. In the past two days, they'd discovered the missing diamond bracelet in a resale shop. Ivan had been right. Someone had strategically targeted tourists during their visit.

On the second day of the investigation, he received an email from Lucia.

The only recent photos I have of the necklace are ones with my mother, Rowan, before she passed away. I hope they lead to its safe return.

— Lucia

Curious, he'd searched for Rowan Starling on the internet and came across the obituary. He read it in its entirety. He was filled with shame to learn Rowan had passed away the week before. Lucia's irritation—her outrage—was like a key sliding into place. He'd falsely assumed she'd been seeking insurance money with the necklace, and he'd been wrong. The last of her mother had been stolen, and Lucia had been stuck with *him* to help her. For two days, he'd felt like a liability to the entire workforce, and Costa had grown tired of his own inadequacy. He hated waste and felt as if he was the waste. He wanted to be better. Costa began following multiple leads to help locate Lucia's mother's necklace, including setting up an interview of the clerk who'd been on shift the day of the robbery.

"Can I help you, sir?" asked a petite and polite woman in a crisp navy pantsuit. She wore a curious expression and a round metal name tag labeled *Sofia*. Her blonde hair was a soft shade of sun.

"Yes. I'm with *Polizia Municipale*," Costa introduced himself. "The owner and I spoke. I'm here to speak with staff who worked the day a robbery occurred."

"Mr. Rossi called me," said Sofia, nodding. "He said we would be seeing you sometime today."

"Why don't we take a seat? I have a few questions."

Sofia gestured to the sofa and chairs in the lobby. She whispered to a colleague who was assisting an older couple. Costa understood the need for discretion. Sitting opposite Sofia on a sofa, he removed a notepad and pen. Flipping a few pages, he poised his pen where he'd left off.

"I'm here to discuss the burglary of a guest named Lucia Starling. She was staying in ..." he checked his notes, "room 424. Can you tell me about her visit? Do you remember when she arrived?"

"It was on Tuesday evening around 19:15," said Sofia. Her hands were folded in her lap as she frowned in concentration.

"How many suitcases did she arrive with?" asked Costa.

"I'm not certain." Sofia appeared thoughtful, considering. "Just the one suitcase, I believe."

"Did you notice her wearing a necklace?"

"I did," said Sofia, her smile evaporating. "It was beautiful. I'd never seen a necklace with that style or color. I was sorry to hear it'd been taken."

"Did you see her coming and going often during her stay here?"

"Yes," she affirmed. "It's not uncommon for guests to have sporadic schedules while they visit."

"Hmm." Costa took note.

"She was quite private, too."

"What do you mean?" he asked.

"Sometimes guests tend to be a bit chatty when they travel through, sharing where they came from or asking for advice about what to see during their stay. She didn't ask for anything."

"Were there any other conversations you had with her?"

"Not really," Sofia shook her head. "Although, she was polite. She would wave the few times she came in or out of the hotel. Though it was odd when someone inquired after her."

"Someone asked about her?" Costa looked up. "Why was this not mentioned the night of the reported robbery?"

"The owner only just mentioned you would be coming to speak with me today," said Sofia, leaning back at his harsh tone. "This afternoon is my first shift since that night."

Costa flipped through his notes. "She was traveling alone, correct?"

"Yes."

"What did this person want with Ms. Starling?"

"Her room number, which is against policy."

His jacket zipper ruffled at his movement. "What was the reason?"

"I was told it was to surprise Ms. Starling with some champagne. Something like that," said Sofia. "The conversation ended shortly after; another guest was asking for some assistance."

"Did you get his name?"

"No name, but it wasn't a—"

"Can you describe features?" Costa pressed hurriedly. "Distinctive clothing?"

"A white shirt, red hair, and a foreign accent. But—"

Costa's pen had paused writing. "Accent? Did it sound familiar? Perhaps he was Austrian or Polish or—?"

Sofia interrupted Costa. "I never said it was a man."

Chapter Twenty-Six

Victor's voice, amiable and smooth, was startling. Her vision was a tunnel of fluorescent light, crowds pressing in, and him. She was going to kill him.

His expression faltered the moment he recognized her. "Woah!" He took a step back as she lunged at him. Oliver quickly pulled her back by the shoulders.

"I won't let you get away with what you did!" she shouted.

"Wait—you're the American woman from Rome! How did you—" Victor's eyes bugged out. "How do you know each other?"

Oliver was panting slightly from the force of keeping her from lunging again. Victor's shocked appearance reflected Lucia's own. His eyes flitted between Lucia and Oliver. She smoothed out her shirt and said to Oliver, "I'm fine. I won't attack again."

"The better question is, what are *you* doing in Amsterdam?" asked Oliver.

"I, uh, erm ... " Victor appeared sheepish before clearing his throat. "I'm in Amsterdam to see that woman."

"Do you mean Mia?" asked Lucia, irritation and fury curling off her in waves. She kept her hands clenched at her side.

"How the hell did you know her name?"

"We were going to find you in Berlin," said Oliver, his voice cutting through the discordant sounds of travelers and gate announcements.

"Well, how did I get so lucky?" said Victor sardonically, kicking his bag at the ground like a soccer ball.

"I discovered your train ticket at my hotel in Rome," said Lucia, pointing at him. "I ran into Oliver on a train headed to Stockholm to find *you*."

"But that doesn't explain how you know about Mia," said Victor, scratching his neck.

"We saw her," replied Oliver. "In the city. She suggested you'd taken Lucia's necklace after recognizing Lucia outside her hotel."

Victor's mouth fell open, jaw ajar. "No. Wait—you're serious?"

"As serious as my mother is dead," Lucia hissed.

"Is she ... always this morbid?" asked Victor, nervously glancing at Oliver before turning to Lucia. "I'll try again—why do you think I stole your mother's necklace?"

"You commented on it!" Lucia sputtered. "That necklace was stolen from my hotel room only hours later. There's really no other explanation!"

"Woah, okay. Okay." He held his palms face up, shifting slightly as people milled around them. "I can explain that part. I only commented on your necklace because I'd seen it before."

Her lungs emptied out. "What?"

"In Stockholm. I couldn't remember at first, but I'd seen it at an exhibition about twenty years ago. I was with my father," said Victor. He gave Oliver a fleeting glance. "The weekend before he'd died ... so I remember everything from that time."

Lucia's thoughts rapidly fired. Her mother had lent the necklace for an exhibit, but only once. In Stockholm, nineteen years ago. "But Mia—she ... " Lucia started.

"She told us you'd recognized Lucia and probably followed her," finished Oliver.

"Mia told you that?" Victor blinked, inflicted. "She told you that I followed Lucia into her hotel and took the necklace?"

She watched Victor's expression of confusion unravel into hurt. It startled her out of her anger.

Then, he began laughing. Low at first, but the laugh, rich and sincere, conveyed how he felt about it. He placed a hand against his stomach. "You thought that I—that I—" he could barely finish before laughing again.

"Care to elaborate?" asked Oliver.

"You thought I broke into a hotel room, " Victor abruptly stopped, running a hand in his hair, "and stole a necklace while on a trip with—*let's not forget*—my cousin, who's a decorated detective?"

Lucia's phone vibrated in her pocket. Her stomach dipped at the sight of the Italian country code. She ignored it for a beat, thoughts tripping over themselves to make sense. "You didn't steal it."

Victor cocked his head at her.

"You didn't steal the necklace," repeated Lucia. Each time she said it made it more true.

Her eyes went to Oliver first, then her phone.

"Do you need to answer that?" asked Victor.

Turning away from Oliver and Victor, she pressed a finger to her ear, answering. Behind her, she could hear them faintly speaking to each other. "Lucia speaking."

"Ms. Starling, this is Costa. I'm the officer who filed the report about your mother's necklace. I wanted to update you."

Her heart thudded in her chest. "Yes?"

"We have a primary suspect."

Everything in her grew cold—not in hope, but dread.

"We are confident of this. However," said Costa. "We discovered recently that this person is possibly tied to several other thefts in Rome."

"Others?" she asked.

"Your robbery is connected to numerous other related crimes in the area. We've determined who likely broke into your room."

Behind her, Victor said, "I still don't understand how we're all here."

"It's a long story," said Oliver.

Lucia hung up, turning toward Victor and Oliver. "I know exactly what happened."

Chapter Twenty-Seven

She brought them up to speed as Oliver flagged a taxi outside the airport.

"The officer was very specific: it was a woman. He described Mia in near-perfect detail," said Lucia.

"I always did make shit friends," said Victor bitterly.

Piled into a cab, Lucia sat at one door and Victor at the other. A flurry of rain pelted against the window, forming rivulets of imperfect lines. Costa confirmed that a woman had pressed the front desk clerk for Lucia's room number in Rome, claiming to be a friend. After the clerk refused to provide the room, the woman—Mia—had somehow correctly guessed which floor Lucia was staying on. Still refusing to give her the room number, the clerk lost track of her after other guests approached the counter. Costa had confirmed identifying details of a tall, short-haired redhead with an accent.

Heading back into Amsterdam in a cab, a catchy commercial for yogurt played on a screen in the front.

"So you two were on the same train," said Victor, whistling. "That's a bit crazy."

"Yes," said Lucia, glancing at Victor. " I actually, um, accused him of stalking."

His eyes narrowed. "But weren't *you* the one going to—"

"*Stalk*-holm?" asked Oliver.

"Wow," said Lucia in admiration. "What a missed opportunity."

"I suppose," said Victor, "this all could have been prevented if I hadn't introduced myself to Mia."

"Speaking of which—" interjected Oliver.

"My missing debit card?" asked Victor.

"Would explain it," nodded Oliver.

"It would. She would've had it for days."

"Which explains the receipts Lucia found," said Oliver.

"It's the only explanation," said Victor, throwing his hand in the air.

"What about the dispensary?" Lucia interrupted their conversational shorthand.

"Now doesn't seem like a great time to stop and pick up weed—" said Victor hesitantly.

"Not for *me*," said Lucia, hand gripping the door handle at a sharp turn.

"Listen, I don't need insults right now—"

Oliver interrupted between them. "What Lucia's trying to say is that Mia told us she works at a dispensary." He took out the business card Mia had given them from his wallet and passed it to Victor.

"I've never realized until now how much of a middle child you truly are," said Victor. He turned the card over in his hand before placing it into Lucia's outstretched palm.

"Mia told me she was a local designer. Now I'm doubting everything." Victor bit at a fingernail, regret on his face. They'd both been conned by Mia; she had taken more than one thing from each of them. The business card was a thick cardstock with a minimalist logo on the front. She read aloud the address and phone number listed.

"There's a way to find out." Grabbing her cell from her bag, she dialed the Netherlands country code and the phone number. As it rang, she gave the card back to Oliver.

"Allo!" A woman's upbeat voice answered. "Budding Boutique, dit is Monica."

"Hi, Monica. I need to speak with someone. Is Mia there?"

"I'm sorry, Mia?" asked the woman with confusion.

"Mia. Red hair, tall like a model."

"Ah, so sorry," Monica laughed. "We don't have anyone who looks like that here."

"The owner's name is not Mia?" asked Lucia.

"No, the owner is a couple named Lotte and Tess."

"My mistake. Thank you for your time." She hung up the phone. Clouds rolled in the distance as they passed street signs and people in the street.

"No one named Mia works there or owns the dispensary."

Victor groaned, sinking into his seat.

"Let's get to the hotel and think," said Lucia. "Once we're hands-free with our luggage, I think we should go straight to her flat."

"I'm down for an ambush," agreed Victor. "I have some things to get off my chest."

Pulling up to the hotel, the taxi parked against the curb.

"I also suggest we call the local police," Oliver proposed.

"I am shocked by your suggestion," said Lucia with a straight face.

"I keep telling him the police are not as helpful as he thinks they are," added Victor.

"They were practically useless in Rome," Lucia muttered.

Oliver gave a sigh between them.

Chapter Twenty-Eight

I n the past hour, Samaran had made several calls while pacing in front of the cafe. After seeing the two leave, he'd taken a chance by making contact with hotel staff.

Despite the reference to Oliver's full name, the hotel had refused to provide a name on the reservation, regardless of his badge. He'd extracted the bare minimum: the woman, an American, had checked out permanently with Oliver, departing in the cab he'd seen. He'd followed Oliver from that night outside the club, hadn't he? Then again the next day, outside that same hotel. Samaran's thoughts emitted self-doubt. Had something happened in between?

Samaran had been arrogant to think his assumptions wouldn't potentially cost him the job. He was properly pissed. As a man with secret gambling debts, he was desperate to pay them off. Accepting the case, he'd assumed it would be a simple catch-and-deliver. Instead, he'd traipsed across multiple countries. He was beginning to feel further and further from recovering his client's items. His restlessness and doubt were persuasive merits for another cigarette.

Removing his coat off a chair, he pulled it over his shoulders. He'd have a final smoke before it began to pour again, and then he'd need to head to his own hotel to figure out the next step. The lighter's flame at his fingertips offered a brief respite from a slight chill in the air. Clicking it shut, he returned it to an inner pocket. Inhaling, he lifted his gaze up to the darkened sky. A young girl with her parents gave him a dirty look as they walked directly in a puff of white smoke. He ignored her.

Leaning against the cafe's stone exterior, still in view of the hotel, a scene in front of him came into sharp focus. He spotted the woman and the man again, this time getting out of a cab. At the sight of a third figure, he pushed off the wall, stunned. *Bloody hell.*

He instantly understood: there were two Swedes, and only one of them had been with Mia.

CHAPTER TWENTY-NINE

They returned to the hotel as rain made its slow descent into Amsterdam. Oliver reached for his bag and Lucia's luggage from the trunk of the taxi. Victor stepped out, shielding his face from a light drizzle. Lucia ducked for cover under the hotel's awning.

"I'll see if I can reserve two available rooms again," said Oliver, shutting the trunk. "Victor and I can share one with double beds if needed."

"Like the sleepovers of our youth," Victor bantered.

"Except this time, we can drink bourbon," replied Oliver. "Mind paying the fare?"

Victor finished paying the driver, but Oliver watched his attention drift over the car and turned. A man in military boots was sauntering toward them, a hard-to-read expression on his face. His darker features, with raven hair slicked back, seemed familiar to Oliver. Water curled against the curb as the taxi pulled away. At the edge of where the street and sidewalk met, the man paused. His attention was hyper-focused on Oliver and Victor.

"I'm Samaran," said the man. "I didn't mean to startle you."

"Who are you?" asked Lucia, more curious than afraid.

It immediately registered to Oliver where he'd seen him. "You were the one following me in Rome."

"Following you?" asked Victor, moving to stand beside Oliver. "Is this someone from one of your cases?"

"Could I suggest we step inside? Perhaps somewhere a bit more comfortable," said Samaran, his British accent thick in the increasing downpour. "I think it would go a long way to explaining everything."

"Here is fine," said Oliver flatly.

Samaran pulled out a badge and handed it to him. Oliver held it at the edge to read it, his gaze narrowing. "You're a private investigator."

"Yes, I am," said Samaran.

"Let's go inside where it's dry?" Lucia suggested, gesturing towards the hotel. "I'd like to hear what he has to say."

In the corner of the near-empty hotel restaurant, the four of them sat. Victor eyed Samaran while Lucia and Oliver sat across from them. Samaran's coat was soaked at the neck, but he hadn't bothered removing it. A table was set, covered in clean white cloth and scattered coffee cups. At the third sugar packet Lucia tore open, Victor gave her a skeptical look. "Is that still coffee?"

Her eyes flitted up, and she gave a graceful lift of her shoulders. Oliver eyed the empty sugar packets as he leaned forward, his attention fixed on Samaran. "Talk."

"I wasn't following you because of one of *your* cases but one of mine," said Samaran. "I was hired a week ago by a gallery owner in Copenhagen. She retained my investigative services due to the high value of her paintings and one emerald bracelet, which had been stolen from her gallery four days before."

"An emerald bracelet?" asked Lucia, head whipping to Oliver. "I saw that on—"

"Mia," breathed Victor.

"We saw it—we saw her just yesterday," said Lucia.

"The majority of cases I handle involve knowing *who* I'm tracking," said Samaran matter-of-factly. "In this particular case, I even knew *where* she would be in Rome. I was hired to bring her in and work with local law enforcement to recover the stolen goods."

"How did that even happen?" asked Victor.

Samaran turned slightly. "She was an assistant to my client and went by the name Clara. I've since learned she's held a variety of identities supported by false documentation, but Mia is her actual name. I monitored her location for two days." Samaran took a sip of coffee, gently pressing a folded napkin to his mouth. "But it's never easy tracking someone who has practice disappearing. She never uses cards under her name. When a source close to her informed me of Mia's whereabouts in Italy, I went there. And I spotted one of you, though I'm still not sure who." His attention went between Oliver and Victor.

"Wait—you're telling me that we were *all* at the same nightclub on the same night?" Lucia interjected.

Oliver's fingers tapped the table as he put the pieces together. "You must've seen Mia approach me when I was at the table alone. I left before Victor and Mia were seen together, which was likely when you followed them thinking—"

"That you were the same person. Yes." Samaran gave a nod. "The next day, after I'd followed them to the hotel, I approached staff for information." At Oliver's incredulous expression, Samaran said, "Rest assured, hotel staff in Rome were fairly tight-lipped. I only got a name. Yours. I, erm, placed an alert on Oliver's card, thinking I'd find the man I'd seen with Mia that night."

"You shouldn't have been given a name in the first place," Oliver's voice was low, on edge.

"It's not personal, it's the job," said Samaran defensively. "You, of all people, should know that."

"You know, I think I get it," said Lucia. At Oliver's dubious expression, she said, "It's true, you could almost be brothers."

"We get that a lot," said Oliver and Victor simultaneously.

"How adorable," teased Lucia.

Oliver's eyes narrowed at first but darted to her mouth at the smirk forming on her lips. Victor held back a laugh, noticing. Lucia's attention turned to Samaran. "It was you, wasn't it—last night on the hotel floor, I thought someone was following me."

"I was searching for him." Samaran pointed to Oliver first but, confused, redirected to Victor. "Sorry, lads."

Oliver clenched his jaw, displeased. "So why approach us now?"

"I thought following you and Mia would be a solid move to

recovering my client's stolen artifacts. Seeing you both out front together, I realized the mix-up. And I ... can't lose this client or this job," said Samaran with a note of sheepishness. "I need your help finding Mia."

"That's exactly what we came here to do," said Lucia. "Mia stole my mother's necklace. I'd thought it was Victor, but that's a much longer story. It was her—it had to be. What I still don't understand is how she found my hotel room in Rome to begin with."

"Ah yes ... well." Victor cleared his throat. "About that."

"About what?"

"She knew about you and—and the necklace because of me," said Victor, chewing his lip.

"Help it make sense," said Lucia, mystified.

"After the book incident, I had plans to meet Mia. We were saying goodbye after drinks when I happened to see you. You were about to walk into your hotel, and I made a passing remark about your necklace. That it—it was like something belonging in a museum. That's actually when I remembered where I'd seen it before," said Victor, distress on his face. "Mia must have followed you after I left."

"Victor, do you know where she's staying?" asked Oliver.

"Yes, it's not far from here."

"If you have that address," said Samaran, "I'll contact local law enforcement now. But we need a plan to prevent her from knowing what's coming."

"If we're going to do this, we need to hurry," said Lucia. "She told us Victor wouldn't return from Berlin until tomorrow. Except he's actually here, so it was all a ruse. I want to get that necklace before anything happens to it." Time was a ticking bomb on the verge of collapsing if they didn't act now. She laid her palms flat on the table and exhaled. "Here's what I suggest we do."

CHAPTER THIRTY

"The place is a huge, open loft in the Westerpark neighborhood," said Victor after giving the cab driver the address. As the driver pulled away from the curb, knots of anticipation twisted in Lucia's stomach. Oliver peered at her, but she turned to stare out at the damp world of the evening. Her mind raced. Adrenaline coursed through her body at the prospect of not only *confronting* Mia but what might come of it. Did Mia still have the necklace?

Anticipation was like standing at the cliff of a canyon and surveying her choices at its rim. When the taxi turned onto a street, the driver slowed in front of a house with one light on.

"It's right here," said Victor, pointing. A light drizzle began to cover the cab window in a watery mist. It was difficult to see clearly, but beyond Victor's side of the taxi, Lucia could make out the shape of a person. Twenty feet away, a woman was closing the front door to a three-story flat. Lucia squinted.

"That's Mia!" exclaimed Victor in a loud whisper.

Before anyone could stop her, Lucia thrust her door open to the rain and the night. Making her way across the street, her steps were light, undetectable. Mia's back was still to her, oblivious. But the sound of the cab door closing prompted her to turn. Victor stepped onto the curb beside Lucia. Mia's eyes darted between Oliver, Lucia, and Victor. Her expression went razor-sharp at the sight of them together. Calculating. A half-second too late, Lucia realized there was a wide gap between her and Victor.

Mia was quick. She shoved through the gap, sweeping past the graze of Lucia's hand reaching out in desperate to grab her. Lucia had assumed her instincts—motivated by the theft of her mother's necklace—would make her fast. But Oliver was faster. Like lightning, he ran.

Lucia's legs sped up to stay close, keeping her eyes on him. Shock mixed with adrenaline as they chased Mia through the streets of Amsterdam. The city at night was a hazy motion picture.

"*Heya!*"

A door to a shop opened without warning, and Oliver nearly ran into a man yelling out. Ahead of them, Mia rounded a corner. Oliver was much closer than she was and gaining on Mia. When she turned the corner at least ten seconds after Oliver, she found him confronting Mia, whose back was to a brick wall of a dead-end. Lucia noticed Mia's hands stay gripped on the bag across her body. They had known this was a possibility. Now Samaran just needed to do his part.

Mia's red hair clung to her cheeks as she faced them, panting. Briefly attempting to push past Oliver, he grabbed both her wrists with one hand as she threw a kick. Twisting, she landed a foot against his right hip. A hand pulled out from his grasp. Stumbling back, a gun in Mia's hand glinted in a street lamp above them. No more than a few feet behind him, she aimed it at Oliver. At the cock of it in his ear, he froze. With his hands in the air, he turned slowly, his eyes on Lucia, who stood at the mouth of the alley.

"I didn't want to do this," said Mia, "you could have just left it alone—"

It happened fast—Oliver ducked his head forward with a jolt. The powerful strike of his right hand cuffed her wrist. His backward motion jostled Mia's hold on the gun. His arm lowered over hers with force, his body facing their hands, which were both wrapped around the gun, aimed at the sky. She struggled, each of them wrenching for control.

Just then—a shot ricocheted.

For one deafening instant, everything launched into the air as if drawn from a bow: the loss of her mother, the necklace, a train ride to a destination she might never go. If something happened to Oliver, she was afraid she'd never catch her breath. It would fly out like an arrow, shooting past her for miles and miles.

Finally, Oliver's left elbow met Mia's nose. Her posture lowered as she moaned in pain, her arms bending at Oliver's grasp. The barrel was covered by his hand, which was almost larger than the gun itself. Getting control of it, he rotated inwards, forcing Mia to lose balance. She was pressing her hands against her nose, bleeding. Pushing the magazine release, Oliver tossed it to the side. He pulled the slide to clear the chamber. Keeping his eyes on Mia, he placed the gun on the ground and kicked it gently toward a wall. The gun scratched the ground in its trajectory.

"Grab it, Lucia," said Oliver, panting lightly.

She reached down to pick it up. Oliver was staring down at Lucia's trembling hands. "What do you need a gun for, Mia?"

With blood gushing out of her nose and her baleful expression, Lucia thought Mia looked frightening. At the sound of heavy footfalls behind her, Lucia turned to find Victor. He stepped close with a whisper only she could hear. "Less than ten minutes. Was that a gunshot?"

Lucia nodded, indicating Mia's gun in her hands. "It's empty," she said. "Oliver has the parts with the bullets."

Victor's eyes were wide. He gently took it from her and put it against the wall behind him. In the distance, cars sloshed into puddles forming in dips in the road. Oliver pushed Mia against the wall in a flash and placed her hands behind her bag. Victor rushed forward to grab the bag that Oliver had managed to remove from her.

"Don't fucking touch it!" shouted Mia, but she was shoving with less resistance. Handing the bag to Lucia, she unzipped it. She rummaged through its contents before throwing it to the ground. "Where is it, Mia? Where's the necklace?"

"Go fuck yourself," she snarled.

"If you promise to be done with your tantrum," said Oliver, his tone casual as if discussing the temperature, "I'll let go."

She stopped struggling. "Fine."

Oliver inched forward, speaking into Mia's ear, though Lucia could barely hear him. "If you try anything, I'll show you just how serious I am about making sure you never get out of prison."

Oliver released her hands and retreated two steps. The three of them blocked the only way out of the alley. Lucia could see the rise and fall of Mia's breaths. She wiped her nose, the blood having slowed. Mia's eyes flickered to Victor. Something close to remorse framed her eyes before it disappeared.

"If you tell law enforcement I cooperated, I'll tell you what you want to know."

"He *is* law enforcement, you asshole," hissed Lucia.

Slowly, Mia's shoulders began to lower. An expression of resignation pulled at the corner of her mouth. Blocked off by the wall, there was nowhere for her to escape. Mia took a breath and let it go.

"I'll tell you what happened."

CHAPTER THIRTY-ONE

Mia sat with a glass of crisp white wine on a terrace, mopeds buzzing by. Tucking a strand of red hair behind an ear, she adjusted the front of her white collared shirt. Her fingers lingered on the emeralds of the bracelet she wore.

Her bracelet, now.

Sure, maybe it had once belonged to someone else. What did it really mean to have something belong to you anyway? Her philosophy was that if you had it, it was yours. She wasn't a hypocrite; if someone stole something of hers, then she'd abide by the rules. Not that she would ever let *that* happen.

She had lived her life without strings and without loyalty for as long as she could remember. Loyalty, she knew, was how her mother had become penniless, full of God and faith and empty pockets. Waiting for someone to save them.

Mia never wanted to go back to waiting or religion. She would become her own God. You only had what you believed in, and Mia believed in herself.

She spotted Victor and gave a wave. He carried a leather-bound book in his hand and had an irascible scowl on his face. He maneuvered around other patrons sitting at round, quaint tables. It was a shame she'd have to get rid of him soon, as she found him to be distractingly attractive. It had been a while since she'd been with a man who complimented her relentlessly. She figured it was only a matter of weeks before he would bore her, maybe sooner. Eventually, it would just be her again, and that was as it should be. So what if she took a slight detour?

"Something the matter?" asked Mia. Obliging, she leaned her cheek toward him for a kiss, his lips warm against her skin. Taking a seat beside her, he ran a hand through his hair.

"Some American spilled espresso on the book I came here for. I was set to sell to a collector in a few days."

"How awful," said Mia. She didn't really care but feigned sympathy. "Should we order some wine?"

"Maybe something stronger," said Victor. He grabbed the attention of a waiter. After placing an order, Mia internally rolled her eyes in exasperation at his distress.

"What does this mean for you now?" she asked.

"It'll be extra time and expense to color-correct some of the pages," said Victor, a hint of uncertainty in his voice. "The buyer will have the final say, but he is aware it was in a slightly vintage state."

Mia clapped her hands together. "See, it's still possible it'll be okay."

"I wish I'd dropped it off at the hotel before meeting Oliver," said Victor with a sigh. He leaned over to kiss her on the neck. "Has anything exciting happened since I saw you this morning?"

"Well, I'm going to Amsterdam tonight. But I had an idea," said Mia, tracing a finger coyly up his arm. "Perhaps you'll come with me."

Victor stared at her as the waiter placed two glasses in front of them. "You want me to come to Amsterdam with you? Tonight?"

Mia stiffened, now marginally doubtful. She'd felt certain he would give an enthusiastic yes, hoping to revel in his attention and good sex for a few more days.

"It was only an idea," said Mia, waving her hand dismissively. "I'll probably be busy anyway—"

"It's a spectacular idea," said Victor with a grin. "Really. When do we leave?"

She laughed and let herself be pulled into him as he placed an arm around her chair. "Meet me at the airport later. The flight departs at 19:30."

He pulled out his phone and scrolled. After two clicks, he put his phone on the table and took a congratulatory sip. "I found it. There was only one flight out of Rome to Schiphol airport at that time. I can meet you at the gate a half hour before it boards." He seemed excited and happy.

It's just a silly affair for a weekend.

But Mia returned the grin. After another glass and conversation about possible evening plans in Amsterdam, they kissed goodbye on the sidewalk. Mia returned Victor's passion, slipping one hand up his neck to kiss him as her other hand slipped into his back pocket.

Palming his card, she could tell it was wrapped in a ticket of some sort. She could feel the energy of his embrace, his longing.

Mia slid the card into an outside pocket of her satchel. The movement of adjusting the gold chain strap onto her shoulder hid the maneuver. As he drew away, Victor's attention narrowed to something over her shoulder.

"That's her, that's the American!" he exclaimed.

A slender woman with long, dark hair crossed the street. She was far enough away not to hear them.

"I suppose Rome is small this way," said Victor. "You should have seen her necklace, though."

"Oh?" asked Mia, her curiosity hooked.

"It reminded me of something I'd seen in a museum," said Victor. He lightly smacked his forehead. "*That's* where I'd seen it."

Mia didn't comment, instead squeezing his hand. "We should go pack," she said with a wink. "You'll get more of me later."

"See you in a few hours," said Victor with a final kiss. She watched him head in the other direction to his hotel.

Spinning on her heel, she hoped she hadn't lost too much time. Speedwalking to catch up to the woman, she checked to find Victor disappearing at a nearby intersection. Once inside, the hotel was quiet, charming. Ahead, she could see the woman carrying two shopping bags in her hands.

Feeling confident in the plan that lay before her, Mia fixed her hair and adjusted the strap of her handbag. A female staff member greeted her with a polite expression. Her metal name tag read *Sofia*.

"Excuse me," said Mia, "I want to surprise a friend with a bottle of champagne, but I've *completely* forgotten her room number." She pretended to be embarrassed with an angled smile. "Could you help?"

"What is your friend's last name so I can find her room?"

Mia's eyes narrowed, accidentally letting her contempt come through. "She's finished medical school, and I want us to celebrate properly," she improvised. She relaxed her expression as quickly as she could. "I'm not sure which last name she gave for the reservation."

"Do you know the floor?" Sofia asked as a phone rang at the desk. "Sorry, one moment, please."

As the clerk spoke on the call, Mia could see the elevator doors slowly closing in front of the woman with the necklace. An arrow above the doors lit up the number four like the hand of a clock. Sofia hung up the phone.

"It's important that it's a surprise," Mia pressed. Time was running out. "She's staying on the fourth floor."

Sofia greeted two guests behind Mia with a small wave. Mia stepped to block their view, annoyed with the ineptitude of front desk staff who wouldn't accept her story.

"I'm sorry, but for the privacy of all our guests, it is not standard practice to provide information. If you want to ask your friend about her room number, I would be happy to help at that time."

"I'll do that," said Mia with a scowl.

Sofia nodded with a polite smile, greeting an older couple behind

Mia. Walking briskly in the direction of the elevator, she checked that Sofia was in assist mode, pointing on a map. At a set of stairs, Mia dipped out of sight.

Yes yes yes.

Running up two steps at a time, she reached the fourth floor panting. On the stairs landing, she reached into her bag to withdraw a small case of electrical tape. Ripping it with her teeth, she tossed the case into her bag. The piece of tape was no wider than her thumbnail.

Checking each corner of where the wall and ceiling met, Mia was gleeful that the entire floor was absent of cameras. Just then, a ding from the elevator sounded.

She hid around the door frame of the stairwell, mostly out of view. The woman she was following carried her shopping bags to a door. A few seconds later, a beeping of the key fob, with two beeps denoting entry. She would have to be fast.

The hallway was empty now except for the sound of the door being pushed open. Mia glimpsed the woman as she set the bags down. Before the door could shut, she swiftly pressed a length of the tape between the door and the frame. For a wild, panicked second, she thought the woman had realized the door hadn't made a sound as it closed.

Although there was always a heady thrill at the risk of being caught, she'd become surreptitious and skilled at burglary over the years. Growing up poor, her youth had been a game of roulette, and she'd grown tired of her siblings with whom she'd been forced to share her food. Resentment had gripped her by the throat. It'd taken decades to shake it loose by leaving it all, and them, behind.

Mia conjured up scenarios for how she was going to successfully steal the necklace from the room without being seen. She considered familiar black market buyers in Budapest she knew would be *very* interested. They were the same buyers who had plans to buy her emerald bracelet in Rome, but their travel plans had changed at the last minute.

Down the hall was a fire exit, its red letters illuminating the shadows where the hallway ended. She made her way toward it.

Leading to the back side of the building, a breeze pulled the door slightly ajar. Her palm pushed it all the way open, allowing her to inspect a rusted fire escape that seemed suspiciously about to collapse. Below was a quiet side street, and she spotted two officers in conversation. Exasperated by the limited options available to her, she reached into her bag, searching for her phone, and all its contents shifted. Folded slips of paper fell from her satchel, landing gently against the wall, out of view.

Mia dared to get closer to her goal of getting hold of the necklace and trailed back the way she came. With an ear pressed against the door, she could hear a shower faucet running.

This is it, thought Mia. She gently pushed the front door open. Water could be heard running, and the terrace doors were open above the busy street. Mia removed the tape, distractedly searching for the necklace. Behind her, the door made a *click* sound of closing. She let out a silent curse. Her heart raced, steam from the shower entering the room. Then, she saw it.

A gold chain with a pendant at its center framed by gold. She traced the smooth blue-green of the jade. Gold glinted in the light. Mia knew by looking at it that it was beyond being defined as vintage; it was exquisite. It was from a different country, a different world, a different time.

Victor was right, the necklace *did* seem like something from a museum. Who was this woman, and why did she have this?

Mia was shocked and delighted. Worth more than money, this necklace could be her ticket to a new life. A life of something more than what it'd been. She'd take it all.

Reaching for the necklace and the passport, she realized the chain was snagged on the collar of the dress. Now was not the time to be partial. She took out a silk scarf before wrapping the passport and necklace with the dress into her bag and hurried out. She knew the woman had to have heard the second *click*.

Running wouldn't help her now; it was too late for that. Hastening, she pulled the scarf over her hair, hiding every last strand of red. She put sunglasses on for good measure just as a door swung open.

Shit shit shit.

Improvising, she leaned into the closed door of a random room. With one hand, she held the doorknob while the other reached into her bag as if searching for a room key. The sound of heavy, distressed footfalls grew closer. Suddenly upon her, the woman was speaking quickly, panic in her eyes. Running out of ideas, she pretended to be a French tourist, balking when the woman spoke in French.

Mia pointed to the fire escape, hoping the misdirection would give her time to get away.

"Merci, merci!" shouted the woman as she ran down the hall.

A few meters away, Mia hurtled herself into the magical timing of elevator doors opening and slipped through. Still wearing the glasses and scarf, she breezed past the busy concierge desk without being recognized. When she was a few blocks away, Mia removed the scarf and pushed her sunglasses over her hair. Pulling the necklace from her bag, her fingers grazed the gold frame as the jade spun in euphoria.

Tucking the necklace into her bag, Mia walked across the bridge, the dying light of day at her back.

Chapter Thirty-Two

Lucia took a step towards Mia. "So where is it? Where's my mother's necklace?"

Mia's lips formed a thin, firm line in the gloom of the alley. Her nose had finally stopped bleeding, but flecks of red mottled her cheek.

Panic clawed its way past Lucia's logic and sense of calm. The hope to get her mother's necklace was more than the necklace itself but about everything it represented: memories and pain and penance and salvation.

Sirens echoed in the distance. Mia started, her eyes darting in the direction behind them.

"What did you do with the necklace?" Lucia repeated forcefully.

"Do you think we're the only ones who were looking for you?" Oliver's voice was dangerous over the sound of dissipating rain. "I know a certain person in Copenhagen who's anticipating a call."

"So what?" Mia jutted her chin haughtily. "Who *cares* about some old art or your stupid mother's necklace? You threatened me, and I defended myself."

Lucia's gaze hardened at Mia's false and desperate attempt to allege innocence.

"Besides," added Mia, "you have no proof."

"Perhaps," said Lucia, leaning in, "you're talking about *this* kind of proof?"

A hand slipped into her jacket pocket. The tension was electric in the small space where they stood. Taking a step back, Lucia held up her phone screen. A series of numbers displayed, and she hit the pause button of the recording. With a press of a button, she sent the file in an email.

Mia's eyes leveled against Lucia, but it was Mia who turned away first. Gradually, the sirens grew louder, a portent moving closer, echoing in the narrow streets until it arrived, blue and red lights dazzling at the mouth of the alley.

CHAPTER THIRTY-THREE

"That was fast," Lucia commented.

Her eyes were trained on Mia sitting in the back of a Dutch police car. Her hands were behind her in cuffs.

"I thought they'd be another ten minutes, at least," agreed Oliver. She peered sideways at him. "I meant you."

Earlier at the hotel, Lucia had laid out a plan: Samaran's part was to notify local authorities as soon as Victor, Oliver, and Lucia left the hotel. He had contacts with the Dutch National Police in Amsterdam and would immediately coordinate with officers to bring Mia in. His client knew the captain of one of the Amsterdam divisions and had made the call. In less than a quarter of an hour, the four of them had leaned over a map, devising strategies and safeguards for where and how they were going to catch Mia. There were at least a dozen factors that could work against them if they were successful in pinning Mia in one location unless they found a way to engage her in conversation. Time would allow Samaran to locate the three of them and summon the police. Lucia shared her location with Samaran, and once he'd verified it was working, they were on their way.

A small crowd had gathered with all the commotion of Mia's arrest. Several saw Mia in the backseat, and strangers craned their necks toward the *politie* car.

Victor sat a few feet away on the wet curb, lost in thought. One of the officers who had arrived with Samaran was in conversation with him. He was tall, with light blonde hair. The second officer stood by the car. Samaran stood with arms crossed, listening. Both officers and Samaran began walking toward Lucia and Oliver.

"With the laws she breached in multiple countries, she'll go away for a long time," said Samaran.

"The recording you sent us is now saved at headquarters, Ms. Starling," said the light-haired officer.

"The recording is essential to the investigation," said the second officer. He stood a little shorter than his partner, with spiky red hair and a more stoic, serious expression.

The first officer added, "We suspect that this is the same woman who has been breaking into flats in the Oud-Zuid neighborhood. We've had many people in the last few weeks report broken locks and high-value pieces gone missing. A few witnesses, but nothing substantial until now."

"Was there any mention of my mother's necklace?" Lucia looked to both officers and Samaran. "Can we determine if she left it at the flat she was staying in?"

For a brief, uneasy moment, the officers glanced between them. "Ah, unfortunately, Ms. Starling," said the first officer, "she claims it's already been sold."

"A buyer?" Lucia choked out. "She didn't say where? To whom?" Her field of vision was a vignette of the world around her.

The officer shook his head. "We will do everything we can to investigate any other information she provides and follow up with you."

Oliver placed a warm hand on her back. He shook the officer's hand with the other.

"You have Lucia's contact information, as well as mine. Please keep me updated if possible."

"Yes, thank you, Detective Ström." The red-haired officer shifted his weight from foot to foot, but it was the first officer who spoke.

"You investigated that case in Stockholm five years ago, right? The unsolved one, with the married man whose wife's niece was discovered in a lake?"

"Yes, I was head of the investigative team."

"Oh, wow!" Wide, admiring smiles broke out from both officers. "How did you do it?"

"Ah, we tracked down old forensics and witness testimony," said Oliver.

"That case went unsolved for ten years. What about the one footprint in cement they found linked to the cousin—"

Oliver politely interrupted by reaching out to shake their hands. "Officers, I appreciate all your help, but we should head out." Oliver kept his palm on Lucia, his fingers making small circles. "It's been a long night."

"Of course. Sorry." The first officer cleared his throat. "We will contact you if we need anything further."

The officers stepped into their patrol vehicle and drove off without the siren, a silent funeral of lights moving past her. Mia did not turn in their direction.

Now that the police car was gone, the crowd's interest had dispersed. The world seemed to resume its orbit.

The spring air smelled of flowers and rain. But it was all *wrong*. Where was she supposed to place the feeling of injustice weighing heavy on her chest? She turned to Oliver, who was shaking hands with Samaran. She glanced at Victor, who was still staring at the road. A conversation with him would have to come later.

"I can make inquiries as to whom and where she sold the necklace," said Samaran. "It might take some time, but after a trial date is set for her, I can work with the attorney who will represent her and—"

"Please," whispered Lucia haltingly.

"It would be no trouble," Samaran continued, "I could—"

"That's not what I meant." Lucia faced him. "Please, don't bother."

"Lucia," said Oliver softly.

"I can't—I won't wait weeks or months, anticipating a phone call only to hear it's gone," she turned to Oliver, her eyes framed in sorrow. "Really gone."

"If you change your mind, you have my contact information," said Samaran, adjusting the lapel of his coat with a nod.

"I won't. But thank you." She squeezed his arm. "I mean it."

His long strides disappeared down the block as he turned a corner. The rain had finally stopped for good. Sidewalks gleamed wet, reflective of shop lights above. Oliver gently turned her to face him. His hands raised from her shoulders to her face. His thumbs, gentle on each cheek, grazed her skin. He never broke eye contact.

Did he know, she wondered, what she was supposed to do now? The finality of so much—her mother, the past four and a half years she and Rowan could've reconciled but didn't, the necklace lost—all shattered together in a blinding constellation.

"I—" she began but stopped herself. She lowered his hands. "A minute," was all she could manage.

Oliver nodded, making his way to where Victor sat. Lucia leaned against a railing in front of a closed flower shop. Families and friends passed her. She barely saw what was in front of her but could see everything from before: before Rome, before her father's phone call, before that final Christmas dinner long ago.

With her mouth tilted to the sky, tears slid in curved lines down the sides of her face, splashing into her hair. She didn't wipe them away. Any motive to find the necklace was crushed by reality, and she was dizzied by a realization:

She was never going to see Rowan's necklace again.

Lucia closed her eyes to the night sky. She whispered her mother's name, half-curse, half-cry, to the brazen, luminous moon above her in devastation.

CHAPTER THIRTY-FOUR

Arriving back at the hotel, they agreed to meet for breakfast the next day. After the night's events, it was clear they were all depleted.

In the elevator, Victor gave a salute before stepping off, his leather backpack slung over his shoulder. "See you in the morning."

From where Oliver and Lucia stood, a mirror hanging on the wall captured a brief picture of them, their shoulders brushing. With last-minute room reservations, their rooms were on different floors. The elevator dinged for Lucia's.

"I'm two floors up," said Oliver. "But can I walk you to your door?"

She agreed with a nod. Silently, they made their way down a long hallway. Locating her room number, she scanned her key fob and pulled her luggage in with her. Oliver propped the door open. She threw aside the fob on a credenza next to the door and flipped on a lamp. Shadows rushed to the corners of the room.

"I'll see you in the morning," said Oliver.

She turned around to face him. "Will you ... " Lucia drifted off.

"Will you stay? Just for a little while."

He nodded, coming in and setting down his bag. "I'll be just a minute," he said before stepping into the bathroom.

He closed the door behind him. Leaning his forearms against the counter, he stared at his reflection. It offered a view of reality: a slightly wrinkled shirt and faint smudges of gray under his eyes. With a deep exhale, he ran the sink water to wash his hands. By the time he walked into the room, Lucia stood in front of the window.

"If you're thirsty." She'd placed a water bottle on a small table behind her.

"I am, actually."

In the culmination of their days together, being alone in her room brought on a closeness he hadn't anticipated. Replacing the bottle cap, he set it on the table. The curtains were open to the city at midnight. Lights glittered around the canals. He met her gaze. She seemed to be waiting for him.

Taking a step toward her, he touched his fingertips to her shoulder, running them up and down her arm.

His eyes sank into hers. "Is this okay?" asked Oliver, his voice hoarse.

"Yes," whispered Lucia, letting out a shiver.

The air was taut with desire to be nearer. Her arms curved around him, bringing him in. He didn't know when it'd started, only that she seemed like a memory to him, something familiar from a past life. Everything between them was built on an afternoon in Rome, giving intimacy a delicate, dreamlike quality. If he admitted it to himself, he'd wanted this from the first sight of her.

She was intoxicating.

She was inevitable.

He leaned down, their lips meeting in perfect symmetry. On his, her mouth was soft after the rain. His fingers rested on her chin. She released a moan, and he stepped closer. Their kiss was newness wrapped in tongue and salt and tenderness. He did not press, did not step closer. He only met her where she was and let her choose the rest. She leaned in, giving him her answer.

***

He'd left her room not long after they'd kissed, but the next morning, when Oliver woke, she was his first thought.

He wanted to call his family. He knew exactly what he would tell them, including, at minimum, setting the record straight on Victor's behalf. After a half hour of phone calls, Oliver made his way down to the hotel restaurant. Victor was already seated against the windows. The wall full of windows opened up to a view of the morning. Other guests made their way to the hotel breakfast buffet.

It was a completely different atmosphere than what he'd experienced at dinner with Lucia two days before.

"Morning," Victor said in greeting with a plate of half-eaten toast and eggs on the table.

"We're speaking English now?" asked Oliver. He lifted his chair out to sit.

"Seems easier to stick to one language while Lucia is with us," shrugged Victor.

"I actually wanted to talk to you about that—" started Oliver.

Victor pointed behind him with a fork. "Speaking of which, she just walked in."

Oliver turned.

He thought she was gorgeous; stunning in evenings, in mornings, and all times in-between. Her long hair was thrown up into a knot at the top of her head, exposing her neck.

"Good morning," said Lucia. She pulled out a chair of her own next to Oliver.

"Would you like any coffee?" offered Victor.

"I can get some in a minute," said Lucia with a smile. "Thanks, Victor." She glanced at the coffee machine puffing and whirring from use.

"How did you sleep?" asked Oliver.

"I don't think I woke up once after my head hit the pillow." She noticed his expression. "What is it?"

"My family would like to extend an invitation to host you in Stockholm," said Oliver. "If you're interested."

Surprise flickered on Lucia's face.

"You spoke to them?" Victor lightly scratched a finger across the tablecloth.

"Both my mother and Linnea. She happened to be there, dropping off Alva and Zuri."

"Oliver's older sister is not my biggest fan," Victor said to Lucia.

On the call with his family earlier, Linnea mentioned wanting to give an apology to Victor, but Oliver kept it to himself until he spoke with Victor privately.

"If you'd like to return to Sweden with us, you can think of it as an extended holiday," continued Oliver. He'd calculated the risk that she might say no against not asking at all. "You would be more than welcome to stay at my flat. I can easily stay at my sister's."

She hesitated, but a flash of eagerness suggested she was considering it. Lucia stood abruptly before saying, "I need coffee," and walked over to the espresso machine.

"Do you think she's okay?" asked Victor.

Oliver watched her go before turning to Victor. "I'm not sure. Also, Linnea wants to apologize to you."

"Does she? I'm surprised." Victor spread peach jam on a piece of toast.

"I talked to her when we first arrived here. Now that we all know about Mia, maybe this will be a chance for things to be different. For all of us."

"Knowing what I know now, I understand why you both thought it was me," said Victor with a sigh. "I don't hold anything against you, especially not Lucia." He seemed to search for what he wanted to say. "I've been running from my father's death for a long time, and what I did to land myself in jail was always going to catch up with me. I hope with time ... you can see there's no secrecy to my life now."

Oliver gripped Victor's shoulder, each understanding the gravity of what was being said. "So. Should I book train tickets to leave this afternoon?" asked Oliver.

"The train ..." Victor appeared bemused. "Oliver, I know you're a famous detective and all, but we might need to knock you out with those kinds of suggestions."

"That isn't the first nor last time I'll be hearing that," said Oliver with a laugh.

Lucia returned with both hands full of coffee and a plate. "Alright," she announced. She sat unceremoniously in a chair, waffles and sunny-side-up eggs spilling around the edges of her plate. "I'll go."

"You'll go with us?" asked Oliver.

"I technically have a flight already scheduled for next weekend."

"A flight from Stockholm?" asked Victor quizzically.

"Yeah ... " Lucia cleared her throat. "This was from plan A, which involved locating you first."

"How many plans were there?" Victor sounded astounded.

"At least four," said Lucia. "In any case, I also still have another few weeks off at the UN."

"As in *the* United Nations?" asked Victor.

She chewed a piece of waffle and nodded.

"Oh, God, Linnea will love you."

Lucia let out a laugh, and its soft chime was so beguiling that Oliver couldn't take his eyes off her.

CHAPTER THIRTY-FIVE

Later that afternoon, Oliver, Lucia, and Victor stood on the platform of the Amtrak station as the train approached.

"How long did you say this trip is?" asked Victor. He turned to Oliver with a bag slung over his shoulder.

"Approximately eighteen hours."

"You're okay with this, too?" groaned Victor, motioning to Lucia. "This old-fashioned mode of travel?"

Oliver could appreciate the sly look she gave, the way her hair fell around her oval face.

"Sure. I've always wanted to experience hours of my life I can never get back."

Victor tossed his head with a laugh. The train doors *whooshed* open along the platform. Oliver waited while several passengers descended before making his way up the steps. Together, they walked in a line of three through the train car. Oliver held the tickets with the numbers of each sleeper carriage. With three rooms booked, the train would be their home for the next day. After their bounty of late breakfast and a shower, Oliver felt better rested for the day ahead.

"Ah, the sweet smell of recycled air," Victor quipped.

Oliver led the way while he checked for room numbers. Burgundy carpet sank beneath his feet, quieting his footsteps. He had booked the overnight rooms relatively close to each other, but it had been tough to get them in the same train car. In the last week he felt he'd checked in, out and slept in enough unfamiliar beds to fill a year. Thoughts of his own flat and his own bed filled his thoughts, and he was more ready to be home than he'd realized.

"It just occurred to me," said Victor to Lucia. "How did you decide Oliver was actually who he said he was?"

"Well, I discovered he wasn't a complete scoundrel when I—"

"—memorized my ID number and verified my identity through Interpol records," interjected Oliver.

She let out a laugh behind him as they arrived at Lucia's sleeper carriage first. He handed her the cabin ticket. She moved against the wall as a few fellow passengers walked past. Their hands brushed.

"Gentlemen," said Lucia before gracefully pulling her suitcase into the narrow room. She peered at Oliver once before closing the carriage door.

"I don't see any gentlemen around here," joked Victor while walking through the restaurant car. Oliver pressed the button for the automatic doors leading to the next train car.

"We're not far from each other. This is you." Oliver handed his cousin the train ticket. "I'm only a few doors down."

"Thanks."

"What is it?" Oliver asked, noticing Victor's hesitation.

"I know I make jokes, but I am glad to be here. Not just with you but with Lucia, too. Having her come with us to Stockholm feels important. I want to explain how sorry I am about everything."

Victor was the closest Oliver would ever come to having a brother. Doubt had put him on a roller coaster, and he was relieved that all that hurrying up for the answer led Oliver to the right one.

Maybe this situation, as terrible as it had been, would repair the wounds in their family. Deep vibrations below signaled motion on the railway track. Oliver peered out the window of the hallway. They slowly pulled away from the platform and out into view of a sunny, clear day.

"See you in a few hours for dinner?" asked Oliver.

"See you," replied Victor, tapping his ticket against Oliver's arm. He shut the door as Oliver ambled toward his own room.

He didn't bother unpacking much except for his toothbrush and a fresh shirt. He frowned at a few of the wrinkles in a button-up. Taking a hanger from the small closet, he hung his shirt around the wooden shape. He sat on the bed as they passed by a red Dutch windmill. The countryside of the Netherlands rushed past.

He felt a text notification from his pocket. It was from Lucia.

He smiled, imagining her squeezing into a bed the same size as his with the same view out her window.

He set aside his phone on a small table in the room. From where he lay on the bed, he could hear the faint squeak of wheels on the tracks. Wind rushed with invisible strength against the window. They'd left the city an hour ago, yet he felt days away from where they'd been in Amsterdam.

For the rest of his life, his heart might pitch over in memory of the gunshot in the alley with Lucia. His relief was still a chill down his spine, fear lingering. He had seen the anguish on her face when they'd learned Mia had sold the necklace and that it was gone, maybe forever. Oliver sat up. Maybe. Or maybe not.

He reached for his phone again, the wind whipping through the trees outside the train as it propelled them toward Sweden.

***

A little over an hour after messaging with Lucia, he splashed some water on his face and changed into a long-sleeved shirt he'd hung in the closet. He walked through a train car in the direction of Lucia's carriage. The restaurant car was filled with groups of friends laughing and a small family reading books at a table. A young girl watched a movie about a singing panda on an iPad. The door *whooshed* open, the car silent again. The door to Lucia's room was slightly ajar.

As he was about to knock, Oliver recognized Victor's voice. He stepped a few feet closer. Victor's low voice could be heard.

"I've often wondered," said Victor, "if it's me. Like I'm a magnet for someone like Mia to latch onto."

"I think it's fair to say you couldn't have known what she was capable of," Lucia said with a note of hesitation. "Listen, I don't mean to overstep, but Oliver told me about your father. I think he wanted me to understand better why my accusations against you were ... complicated."

"He was a complicated man," said Victor, voice heavy with the weight of the past. "There was a lot of fallout after his death. A lot of things I could never get closure for. In Rome, I yelled at you and heard *him*. I felt ashamed to have behaved so much like my father. I'm glad l can properly apologize to you now. I am *really* sorry."

"My mother was complicated, too. Our relationship was really tricky."

Through a small opening of the door, Oliver could see the open expression on her face.

"Did you know she only lent the necklace for an exhibition once?" she asked finally.

"Where? In Sweden?" asked Victor.

"Yes," she nodded.

"Holy shit."

"I know."

There was a long silence. Long enough for Oliver to feel he should turn around and return to his room. Train wheels lightly squealed in the distance. As he began to turn, he heard Lucia speak and stopped.

"At first, I thought my mother left the necklace to me out of some kind of guilt trip for not speaking to her for years," said Lucia. "When it was taken, it felt as if all my memories of her—good and bad—were stolen with it."

"I'm sorry we're both in the dead parent club," said Victor in understanding.

Lucia's laugh was soft. "Yeah, the entry fee really fucking sucks. I'm sorry, too. For, um, stalking you?"

"I've never had a stalker before," chuckled Victor. "I do hope you're the last."

At Lucia's laugh, Oliver retreated to give them privacy, taking the quiet walkway back in the direction he came.

Chapter Thirty-Six

The next morning, the driver pulled up slowly to Oliver's parents' house. It was almost nine. Lucia felt fatigue's heavy hands on her eyelids, pulling them down like shutters. "What is it usually like here in the summers? What time does the sun go down in the evenings?" asked Lucia as they stepped out of the taxi.

Victor shrugged, looking at Oliver. "This time of year? Close to 22:00."

"Sometimes even later," answered Oliver. He swatted her hand away as she reached for her suitcase. As Oliver carried each of their bags out of the trunk, Lucia turned toward the house.

Sleek vertical lines drew her gaze up the length of the house. It seemed a perfect combination of modern style and Swedish farmhouse. The slanted, black roof gave a minimalist feel. Like something from a magazine.

Beneath a bower of trees lay a bed of flowers, the earth softened with color around the siding. It made the side garden, filled with blooming and wild pink flowers, evoke an essence of spring. The *s* shaped path of stones was flanked on each side with blue hydrangeas and led to the wide front door, which matched the color of the roof.

Her mother had visited Stockholm, she remembered. Once, to personally deliver the necklace for the exhibition, and three months later at its close. Until now, she hadn't realized there was another reason she'd said yes to Oliver. The entire trip had become about her mother. Or maybe it had always been. Lucia could feel her here, under the warm evening sun of Sweden.

Around the manicured yard, a woman began to walk toward them. It was easy to guess it was Oliver's mother. Her coloring, paired with light eyes, reminded Lucia of him. His mother was a vision of a classic, motherly appearance. With hair tied loosely in a bun, wisps of blonde at the nape of her neck were a little lighter than Oliver's. In her hands she carried a trowel, which she rested against wide rocks winding along the footpath.

Oliver and his mother embraced. After a few exchanges, Oliver gestured to Lucia.

"Yes, of course," said Oliver's mother with a smile. "I am Elina. I hope you are okay with my rusty English. It's been some time."

"So wonderful to meet you," said Lucia, extending her hand.

"Linnea and Tuva will be out in a moment," Elina embraced Victor. "We didn't know when you would arrive, so we were outside on the deck with some coffee."

"Started without us, I see," said Oliver.

"Oliver!" called out the taller of two women behind Elina. The one who'd called out gave him a hug, her shoulder-length hair framing her face. Lucia did a double take. She was the spitting image of

Oliver in female form.

"You failed to mention you had a twin," said Lucia in astonishment.

"This is Tuva, the youngest of us all," laughed Oliver.

"The architect," Lucia commented with a smile. Tuva's coloring and mannerisms were so like his. Lucia turned to the other woman.

"Which must make you the other—"

"Pain in the ass," remarked Victor, a smile forming.

"That's exactly right." The woman's smile broke out across her face, and she pushed him playfully. "Even though everyone said having kids would change me."

"This is my sister, Linnea," said Oliver. "The smartest one of the group, though unfortunately, it's a low bar."

"I've always been an only child and wished for siblings," admitted Lucia, glancing between Oliver and his sisters. She turned to Elina. "Brave to have three kids."

"Yes," Elina's smile revealed faint dimples as she gave Lucia a wink. "But I only love two of them."

"We all know who she's talking about," said Tuva, who gave Oliver a side-eye.

"You're so confident it's you," chuckled Oliver.

A warm orb of pleasure moved through Lucia in witnessing Oliver with his family. The quiet reservation, his intensity, was still there, but now there was lightness, too. Familiarity melted into openness. She felt a warm glow of admiration and envy.

As they stood on the front lawn talking over and to each other,

Linnea and Victor walked off together in close conversation. Elina had one arm around Tuva, and they followed behind Victor and Linnea toward the patio.

Lucia took it all in. She felt the world narrow down to where she was. Oliver rested a hand on the small of her back, fond and familiar. Her eyes filled with the sight of him.

Her mother would never know this, would never see Stockholm again or the rest of the world. Would never smell flowers in the early summer of Sweden. There were a thousand tiny cuts, knowing her mother would never know this version of her. This person she was becoming and the world she was seeing.

I'm here, his eyes seemed to say. His gaze was steady.

She gave a nod to his unasked question: she was ready. Reaching for her hand, he grabbed her suitcase in the other. They walked together toward the patio covered in trees at the bottom of a hill.

***

Lucia sat on the cushion below an arched window. She'd excused herself to send Simon and Adeline a text in their group chat. Light-hearted conversation drifted in from the next room. Linnea seemed to be giving Oliver a hard time about something, but she guessed it was a natural rapport between them. Oliver's mother sat across from him, sipping her coffee. His arms were crossed thoughtfully as Tuva gestured while she spoke.

As if sensing her, he met Lucia's eyes across the room. Her mouth curved, seeing him. Turning her attention to her phone, she triple-checked the time in New York. She wasn't certain what time zone her father was in, but if he was home, it was the middle of the night. She wanted to let him know she was safe in Sweden.

Their last conversation had been about the two flights out of Schiphol. There was still so much to resolve between them; it might take years. But if they were lucky, they could use that time to mend whatever remained of them as a family.

She typed, biting her lip.

> *I'm safe, currently in Sweden. Are you flying these next few days, or can we talk soon?*

Placing her phone in the outside pocket of her suitcase, she stood and walked into the kitchen. Above her, a wide skylight let in the sun. Victor was making a comment right as she walked in, causing the room to erupt in surprised laughter.

"I was just telling them how Samaran mixed us up in Rome," said Victor, pointing to Oliver.

"That happened all the time when you were children," said Elina. She offered Lucia a cup of coffee, which Lucia accepted graciously.

"You did all of this while I was in the other room?" asked Lucia, taking in the view of a full spread of toasts, jams, meats, cheese, and fruit. Next to the serving dish were large tubes of caviar and a stack of thin, crispbread crackers.

"Our mother always keeps her kitchen well stocked," said Tuva. "Are you hungry?

"Starving," said Lucia with a smile.

The dining table was in a large oval shape, reminding her of the base of a ship. It was made of dark wood, with elegant cane chairs. She sat in the empty chair next to Oliver.

"Your house is incredibly tasteful," commented Lucia with an admiring survey of the space. To her left sat Linnea, who waved a hand to her mother across the table.

"She's very modest, but I think it could be featured somewhere."

"I only chose paint colors. It was Tuva and her father who did the design. He is on his way home from kayaking, so he can tell you all about it," said Elina.

"What is your dad's name?" Lucia asked the siblings.

"Save some for the rest of us, eh?" Victor playfully argued with Linnea, who was serving herself heaps of cantaloupe.

"Never," she gave a wicked grin before handing him the serving spoon. She turned to Lucia. "Our father's name is Issac. He's an engineer in the city."

Lucia listened to the conversation floating around her as she took a bite of her food.

"Linnea, aren't you in the process of another clinical trial?" asked Oliver.

"Right, you're a medical scientist," said Lucia, straightening. "Oliver mentioned it."

"Is that what these men told you?" She waved a fork between Victor and Oliver.

Lucia hesitated, glancing from Linnea to Oliver, and wondered if she'd gotten it wrong.

"These overly handsome buffoons are simplifying a complicated field of study," said Linnea before taking a bite of cheese.

"I resent the implication that my handsomeness is excessive," said Oliver in vexation.

"I am technically a biostatistician," Linnea ignored her brother and answered Lucia. "My master's thesis was about statistical inference as it relates to genetic diseases. Now, I analyze specific genetic factors linked to rare forms of cancers. I've spent the last two years focused on a cardiac form of cancer."

Lucia slowly set down her fork and stared. She suddenly recalled what Oliver had been saying in Amsterdam about his sister's research.

Oblivious, Linnea took a bite from her plate as she continued. "The clinical trial we've held has been in pairs, where we evaluate the genetic mutations, hereditary aspects, and health components that exist within a family. Fathers, sons, mothers, and daughters. We're in the second round of the study, but results have been incredibly dispiriting. The statistical rate of survival of cardiac sarcoma—"

"—in the US is less than forty-seven percent in five years," said Lucia. Her words came out as a loud whisper. "If we're to go by statistics in my country."

"That's correct, how did you—" Linnea stopped, noticing the wordless, aching expression on Lucia's face. Conversation at the table quieted. Linnea recognized the magnitude of the information from the silence.

"Who was it?" asked Linnea gently.

"My mother." Lucia began to reach for her empty collarbone but placed her hands in her lap. "What have you seen indicated in the trials relating to possible improved prognosis?"

Linnea set her fork down carefully, the attention of the entire table on them. Turning to Lucia, her expression was full of reservation. "I'll be frank with you. Results still point to a determination that, due to this rare type of sarcoma, it is resistant to treatment. I am in a lab, so I don't face the families or those with the condition at the time of diagnosis. I see them when they have faced all other viable options. Even then, it spreads quickly. The malignant cells in a sensitive organ like the heart create an inevitable chain reaction, impacting the rest of the body. Unfortunately, in the intervening time of diagnosis to when trials begin ... well, the morbidity rate ... " Linnea reached for Lucia's hands, holding them as she continued.

"Accelerates," Lucia finished for her.

"Due to the nature of this rare type of angiosarcoma, all data points to it being resistant to treatment," said Linnea, nodding. "Surgery gives borrowed time. Not for as long as people deserve."

After her father had called to break the news of Rowan's death, Lucia had spent the days leading up to the funeral obsessively researching. She didn't understand why her mother hadn't told her she was dying. Her mother took away Lucia's chance to forgive her or continue hating her, but at least she would have been given a choice.

Perhaps knowing the margins of survival were statically insurmountable helped her understand, too. She would have become sick very fast. Hearing Linnea's medical perspective took on a different meaning. The information meant something different to her now.

"I'm so sorry," said Linnea, whose voice was thick with the profoundness of the moment. "Your story is why I do what I do. I'll never give up."

She reached for Oliver's hand beneath the table. His thumb grazed her knuckles in slow movements.

"I am here to answer any questions that could possibly help bring you some peace," offered Linnea.

"I—" Lucia began. Uncertainty grew from the place where needing to know had consumed her. "Please forgive me. I didn't mean to change the mood of breakfast."

Lucia wiped at the corner of each eye with her hand. Lucia felt surrounded by understanding and acceptance even though she'd only just met his family. Outside the window, a deer stretched its neck and lingered in the high grass near the patio. The room radiated light. Above her, the skylight shunned every shadow to the periphery of the room. It was Tuva who surprised her, breaking the silence first.

"Grief makes it feel strange to live in this world after someone we love has left it," said Tuva with gentleness. "It tricks us into thinking it replaces the space where love has been."

Victor spoke, his voice uneven with emotion. "We feel sad with you, not for you." He said gently to Lucia, and she knew he, of all people, really understood what it meant to lose someone you thought you could live your entire life without. Only to find the absence of them a deprivation instead of total relief.

Elina nodded in agreement with Tuva's words. Oliver's sister was right; she grieved her mother. She loved her mother.

She loved her mother. She loved her mother.

CHAPTER THIRTY-SEVEN

After dinner, Oliver brought Lucia to his flat. Despite her initial protests, he had offered her his place while she stayed in Stockholm.

Tuva offered Oliver her guest room so Lucia would have his place to herself. She stood on the sidewalk as he pulled out keys to the entrance of his building. It was early afternoon now, teeming crowds of people wandering and socializing. Cafes and parks were filled with families.

Oliver pushed open the door and held it for Lucia. Leading the way up the steps, his right hand carried her luggage. Even after she'd insisted on carrying it herself, he'd put it slightly out of reach. Two flights up, she began to tease him.

"Any regrets yet?"

"No such thing," said Oliver. He didn't even sound winded. Lucia admired the view of his shoulders beneath his shirt while she ascended the floors behind him. Distracted, she missed a step, and her shoe fell hard on the third-floor landing.

"Everything okay?" asked Oliver, glancing over his shoulder.

"Mmhm." She watched her steps a bit more carefully on the last flight of stairs.

When they reached his front door, he lowered her luggage. With a soft *click*, he unlocked his door.

"After you," said Oliver with an outstretched arm.

As she stepped in, her gaze moved up toward the skylight in the entryway. Perhaps the primary perk of living on the top-most floor. Sitting down on the bench, she undid her shoes. The door closed quietly.

She walked barefoot throughout his home, curiosity leading her while she went from room to room. Oliver leaned against a wall between the kitchen and main room, watching her. A smile ghosted his lips. Her fingertips grazed open kitchen shelves filled with ceramic plates and mugs. Everything was neat, organized in clean white lines.

"Where do you eat?" asked Lucia quizzically.

His arms uncrossed as he pushed off the wall. He lowered a safety latch beside the kitchen counter, which turned a food prep surface to form a foldable birchwood table.

Lucia swept her palms across the smooth surface. "Swedish people really have thought of everything."

She stepped into the main room with floor-to-ceiling bookshelves. They were filled with books, sculptures, and photographs. Walking closer, she read aloud the titles on each spine. "Slim Aarons, Peter Lindbergh and ... Patty Smith?" With Smith's book in her hand, she turned to him. "I've always been under the impression that your work was intense and all-consuming. But you have a pretty decent library."

"A good rule is to never trust someone who doesn't have a shelf of books."

Lucia replaced the book on its shelf, gently brushing a finger over the handle of a ceramic vase. A small chip in the wide neck revealed white material. Everything in his home felt lived in, comfortable. Like it belonged.

"Linnea is incredible," remarked Lucia as she lowered to the bottom shelf of books. "How many years apart are you?"

"Five," answered Oliver. His eyes glinted with a smile she'd come to know when he talked about his sisters. "But she's lived a dozen lives while we mere mortals grew up in regular time."

"What do you mean?"

"She volunteered for a summer building houses in Guatemala before going to university," explained Oliver. "She also lived in America for a few years as an au pair in San Francisco. She learned how to surf for a few years."

Lucia rose to her feet. Silence stretched on, neither saying anything.

Oliver gestured to the kitchen. "Would you like some water? Or something else to drink?"

"White wine would be great, thank you." She went to sit on the sofa, plush with two pillows. Oliver grabbed two glasses and went to the drink trolley in front of the main window. He removed a rubber cork from an already opened bottle, pouring portions into both glasses.

"How did she meet her husband? Aaron, right?" asked Lucia as he handed her a glass.

"Aaron and Linnea met when she was working on her first clinical trial," said Oliver. "He's originally from Ethiopia and has been living in Stockholm since graduating from university twenty years ago. We were all replaced as the family favorite once they had their daughters. That's Alva and Zuri." Oliver pointed to a framed picture of two girls hugging each other.

Lucia squinted at the pictures of the girls he referenced on the shelf. With their curly dark hair and wide, laughing smiles, they seemed wild and happy. Sitting together in comfortable silence, they sipped from their glass.

"Your home is really cozy," Lucia looked around at the view from the sofa. "All the light wood and cream color is very calming."

"I think so, too." Oliver's eyes softened. "How long would you like to stay?"

"I fly out in five days from Arlanda. I'd really like to explore the city. Is that too long?" she asked, uncertain. "It's not a problem to stay at a hotel."

"You can stay as long as you'd like," said Oliver, his eyes meeting hers over the glass.

He made so many things seem easy. "Do you like where you live?" asked Lucia.

"I do. Very much," he rested a leg across his other knee. "The location is very close to water, and it's not far from my family. I also don't mind the sounds from the street; it helps me sleep at night."

She imagined it all, the late night laughter of youth, the early sunrises and their golden light between buildings. It made her think of New York City.

"What about you? Do you enjoy where you live?" he returned her question.

"I live in a brownstone in the West Village," said Lucia. She folded her legs underneath her. "I really like the neighborhood. All I know is New York; the city raised me. Even despite the falling out with my mother, my closest friends, Addy and Simon, live nearby. Coming here, seeing the photos on your shelves and the photography books of other countries ... it makes me think maybe I haven't considered if I wanted home to be somewhere else. Perhaps I should." She went quiet, peering into her glass.

"Do you want to talk about her?"

Oliver's question was posed with gentleness, but it was still a dagger. Across the room, her eyes traced art on a wall next to a window. A framed museum poster of a Van Gogh exhibit in Norway hung in the center of the two bookshelves. Everywhere was another place.

"It's hard to explain how I feel about her—because she was my mother, right? She was supposed to act like a mother, not an asshole. But in my life, she's been both," said Lucia with a halfhearted laugh. "From a career standpoint, she was brilliant. She dived into a profession that, as a first-generation daughter of immigrant parents, was risky. She chose something she loved, and she was good at it."

"What about your father?" asked Oliver as he took another sip from his glass.

"He became a pilot young, so by the time I came around, he was pretty established. He used to travel a lot more when I was growing up. He works for a commercial airline now, but I spent a lot of time with my mother because of it. Perhaps my dad expected too much of her," said Lucia, thinking aloud.

"In what way?"

"Well—that she should carry the burden of domestic life while he got to leave." She'd never considered what it must have been like for her mother in that way. Maybe Lucia had been the easier target of her mother's resentments. Her father's career wasn't Rowan's fault, but it *was* her responsibility to be the present parent. Lucia swallowed, setting her hands in her lap. "Your family was very kind to let me cry over the cheese plate."

"You can cry anytime you feel like it," Oliver replied seriously.

"Most men would never say that."

"Most of my world is spent at crime scenes involving pretty heavy stuff. A woman crying is the bare minimum of what I can handle."

Lucia studied him. "You're so different from most men I know."

"You're so different from most women I know."

Four floors down, Lucia could hear people laughing in cafes. She uncrossed her feet and set them gently on the ground. Moving over a few inches, she came closer until her thighs touched the outside of his knee. With a hand on his chest, she leaned in.

The dazzling light of afternoon in the room brought out the fierce blue of Oliver's eyes. In the past week, their hue had changed each time she'd looked. Now, with his body warm and close, his eyes reminded her of a storm out at sea. He kissed her then. His lips were soft, confident. They sank into each other. His tongue lightly traced her lips. Moving her hands from the fabric of his shirt to his neck, she cupped to press him closer. His hands held her face as they leaned in, so close there was no gap between them. It wasn't until he broke them apart to place his lips on her neck that she gasped.

She had forgotten. Forgotten what it meant to be touched. Oliver's gentle sweep of his fingertips on her body spoke to sensuality like it was another language he knew. His lips on the sensitive part of her skin lowered slowly, slowly until he reached her collarbone. Tugging the sleeve of her shirt, he gently pulled it aside until the roundness of her shoulder was exposed. Feeling impatient, she pulled her shirt off and discarded it onto the floor. She removed his shirt and took in the view of him.

He seemed built for her: wide shoulders, thoughtful, light eyes with a penetrating gaze. She wanted more. As she leaned in to meet his mouth, his hands unclasped her pants.

Sliding them lightly down the length of her legs, he lowered himself to remove the final inches between them. He kept his eyes on her as he moved to the floor and kissed her shins, her knees.

"Do you want me to keep going or stop?" asked Oliver softly. His lips grazed the skin of her other knee.

"What?" Lucia was breathless.

"I can stop if you want, if it's too much." He paused to let her answer. His head rested against her thigh, the expression on his face exceedingly patient. As if he would savor whatever part of her she was willing to give and be satisfied.

"Don't you dare stop," rasped Lucia.

He reached for the lace fabric between her legs. His hands, slender and strong, gripped her thighs as he pulled her closer. His lips pressed into the center of her. With his tongue and fingers, he tended to her pleasure. Slowly, his fingers slid inside of her. He hissed at how tight she was, and Lucia sank into what his mouth was offering. Panting, she let her body take over, giving in to the rhythm of what he was doing. She wanted him inside of her, desperately. She pulled at him. With a kiss along her thighs, he moved his hands beneath her to lift her off the couch. He shifted her into his arms as if she weighed nothing.

"I'm too tall to be carried," she laughed.

He did it anyway. Once in his bedroom, he placed her gently on the bed. Outside the window was a warm glow of afternoon coming through the half-opened curtains.

Lucia settled into the pillows as Oliver tossed his remaining clothes to the floor. Lowering himself over her, there was nothing between them now. She pressed herself to him, her nipples tight against his chest.

"I have wanted you since Rome," Oliver's voice was full of tenderness. "I saw you, and it was as if I'd been waiting for you."

Somehow, that day on the train, he'd seen her. *Really* seen her, beyond the hostility and the skepticism while she'd frantically searched for her mother's necklace. Somewhere between mountains and a lake, seeing Oliver felt like a deep kind of recognition. A startling feeling of *there you are.*

He tore a plastic wrapper with his teeth. Wanting him consumed her. As he slowly entered her, she wrapped her legs around his waist, pulling him in. His mouth was warm and searching on hers.

Here was a place inside her she hadn't dared look at for years. They moved, hands intertwined as if they were both afraid to let go. His other hand danced between them, gently coiling her toward a peak of pleasure she ascended with each breath. She wanted him with an intensity built on years of only having herself.

With one final thrust, he tipped her over the mindless edge of pleasure. His arm banded around her waist, keeping her close as if he knew what she was feeling, that he was feeling it, too, and wanted to carry them through it together. Her climax was like free-falling into an abyss, and she pulled him along with her into the void where only they mattered.

With him, she learned there were other ways to drown that had nothing to do with grief.

CHAPTER THIRTY-EIGHT

"Do you think we should let Tuva know you'll be staying here?" asked Lucia the next morning. She rolled onto her side and pulled up the sheet to cover herself.

"Tuva is smart. She'll have figured it out."

He kissed her exposed shoulder. The morning sun offered a golden, radiant hue to the room. Hints of daylight slanted through, creating long horizontal lines across the duvet.

"What should we do today?" asked Lucia with quiet excitement.

"I have a few ideas. One would be to take you to a historic part of the city, Gamla Stan. It's part of the Royal Palace," explained Oliver with a kiss on her palm. "The king's residence is there as well."

"I forget that Sweden has a royal family."

"It's nice. It's near the water," said Oliver. "There's also the Bergius Botanical Garden."

"All very good suggestions." It was nice to realize she had days ahead of her to explore the city. It felt good, energizing. A city she'd never seen and had never expected to, but it felt right.

Oliver was the vision of relaxation. His eyes were closed and his posture was partially upright with two pillows behind him. After a few quiet seconds, one eye opened. She smiled mischievously and slowly crept one hand under the covers. As she inched down his torso, her phone sounded. She was sorely tempted to ignore it but felt she should check in case it was Adeline, Simon, or her father.

"I probably need to … " She drifted off as she searched under her clothes on the floor for her phone. Naked, without a sheet to cover her, she walked in circles. The phone made its repeated chime as she searched.

Oliver gave a warm laugh as she realized the chime was coming from his hand.

"Thank you," Lucia snatched the phone from his hand with a smile of her own. Her father's name flashed on the screen right before it disappeared on the third ring. She'd have to call him back.

As if he knew, Oliver had begun to get dressed. "I'll go get some coffee." He put on jogger pants and a short-sleeved shirt as she reached for the covers for warmth. He gave her a kiss, soft with memories from the night before.

Lucia smiled appreciatively and said, "That would be great." He always seemed to know what she needed before she even had to ask.

Oliver disappeared into the living room, the sound of the front door of the flat closing. She called her father, and he picked up on the first ring.

"Hi, Dad."

"Hi, Lucia. So," said her father, his voice unsure. "You're in Stockholm now?"

"Yes. It's only my first day in the city, so I'll be sightseeing later. I … I wanted to let you know I'll be flying back to New York on Saturday, but I did take a short leave from work until the end of the month."

"I think that's a good idea," he said. "I support it."

"What about you?" Her fingers played with the fabric of the duvet. "Will you give yourself time, too?"

Once, when she was twelve, she'd snuck downstairs at the sound of music in the kitchen early one morning. She'd discovered her parents sitting at the table laughing, their hands folded together on the table in the soft light of dawn. They'd loved each other. They were together long before she'd arrived, but now she and her father were the only ones left.

"Lucia?"

His voice was oxygen to all the memories that had suffocated her for so long. Standing, her feet padded across the floor to stand next to the bedroom window.

"Sorry," said Lucia. Her fingers lingered on the long ivory curtains that dragged onto the floor. Four floors below, a woman crossed the street, her long skirt ruffling in the breeze behind her.

"I was thinking of you and Mom. I just … " said Lucia, her fingers trailing along the sheer fabric. "Can you help me understand why you didn't tell me?"

A sigh, filled with regret and something sorrowful, tinged the roughness of her father's familiar voice. "She was really, really sick for so little time before it got bad," said her father. "I think your mother was selfish about her choice not to tell you after her diagnosis. I wanted to, even though there was so much already between you two. In the end, I think I understood what she was really doing ... she was punishing herself for what she'd said that night. But I should have fought her harder." His voice wavered. "That might haunt me for the rest of my life. Because I hurt you in the process. With our silence, we both did."

Lucia turned, the world of Stockholm laughing and carrying on outside. The phone was silent for a long time.

"I spent so long missing her that it feels awful to give it a name now that she's gone," said Lucia finally. Tears ran in straight lines to her chin. Her hands clutched her phone.

"I wish we both could've had more time. Maybe things would've been different. I'd like to think they could have been."

Time. It cleaved her open to know there was no such thing as time lost, borrowed, or gained. There was only what happened.

"Are you safe?" the tenor of his voice filled with uncertainty.

"I'm safe," said Lucia as she wiped at her cheeks. "I'm sorry if I worried you."

"Good. I wasn't—I suppose I'm still not sure what happened in Amsterdam. I hope you'll tell me when you feel ready."

Tears spilled over as she told him everything. About the robbery in Rome. The police in Italy and her decision to follow Victor. Simon corroborating Oliver. Mia getting arrested. Retelling the events of the past few days eased her shoulders lower.

"Wow—I mean, really, wow," said her father in shock. "You've been through a lot. I'm so glad you're okay, but I'm so sorry about the necklace."

"Can you tell me why she left the necklace to me?" asked Lucia.

"Because you are her daughter," her father's words traveled across an ocean to reach her ears. "It was the beginning of her career, and it was her legacy. You were the only person she wanted to have it."

"And see what happened—" Lucia choked out a sob. "She had it for nearly three decades, and I had it for a week."

"That necklace should have been donated to a museum. It's not your fault. Okay? It is not your fault what someone else did. Your mother should have known better than to burden you with something else."

Their shared grief was like rocking in a small boat, each of them gripping the sides to stay upright while they silently adjusted to the world's sway without Rowan. Lucia heard the front door open and close and Oliver's footsteps in the kitchen.

"I should probably ... "

"It's alright," said her father. "I have a 7 a.m. flight to Seattle. I only wanted to make sure you were okay."

"I will be, eventually."

"What time is your flight out of Stockholm? I assume it's out of Arlanda."

"I don't have it in front of me, but it's an evening flight. Eight-ish."

"Alright, let's talk more once you're home. And Lucia ... " Emotion fissured around her name. "Happy birthday. I don't want you to think I forgot."

After hanging up, Lucia sat on the edge of the bed. It was the first year of the rest of her life without her mother. Thinking of the conversation with her father reminded her of a conversation she'd had with Simon and Adeline a month ago. It had been early April, a warm almost-summer day. Throngs of families were scattered in the grass of a park as the three of them sat on a picnic blanket in full view of the Brooklyn Bridge.

"One of you can be the first," said Adeline, suggesting Lucia reach out to Rowan if ready.

"After everything she said, I really don't think it should be me. Why should I apologize?" asked Lucia stubbornly.

"Maybe she feels ashamed," said Simon in his matter-of-fact way.

"I don't think she's tried to understand you or made much effort," clarified Adeline. "But maybe she was doing the best she could, even if it is profoundly short of what you deserve. Maybe I'm wrong—maybe having her in your life is harmful, and going no contact is best. But what if by reaching out you can give yourself real, true permission to move on? No more what ifs or hope. Just reality. Only you will know the difference."

Coming from her oldest, dearest friend, Lucia tried to withstand sitting in the face of unflinching honesty. At the heart of it, Simon and Adeline only wanted her to be okay. Despite her protests, Lucia did want to open the lines of communication with Rowan—to find out if the years had changed something in either of them. Lucia thought back to all those years ago when she briefly lost sight of her mother at Coney Island. The way fear had grasped her by the throat and stolen her breath, so terrified she'd never find her way back to her again.

Maybe she had become a person her younger self had hungered for: a person who needed her mother but could live with the fallout of not having her. Lucia considered what it might mean to try to reassemble the disparate pieces of each of them. Did it matter if she just ... simply missed Rowan? She was, after all, her daughter. She couldn't hate her mother without hating herself.

Around them, life carried on. Boats across the water. Cars across the bridge. The skyline in the distance reaching towards a blazing, shifting sun. She wanted to call her mother and say, *I have your eyes.*

Maybe there was nothing more to say. Maybe there was too much to say.

Less than two weeks later, her mother died.

CHAPTER THIRTY-NINE

In Oliver's neighborhood of Södermalm, vintage shops and bohemian cafes poured onto sidewalks. Since her arrival two days ago, they'd walked around Stockholm as he shared his city with her.

"I like the neighborhood's relaxed nature," said Oliver. "Especially at night in the summer, the sounds of people in cafes are comforting. People just ... talking about life. What?"

"Wow," said Lucia, reaching up to give him a kiss. "I've never heard you say so many things in a row. Do you mind leaving some words for the rest of us?"

His laugh came out deep and smooth, like a hand running over velvet.

She'd come to appreciate the city as a place where conversation and the sun collided into the late evening. Stockholm was one of the cleanest cities she'd ever been to. It was the alluring sky of early summer in Sweden that Lucia came to love. At times, vermillion streaked the sky like a brush that'd run out of paint partway through.

She'd seen how many people still milled about, even close to midnight. New York was always bustling, even late, but perhaps in the summer, Stockholm was the city that never slept.

On her second day in Sweden, Oliver wanted to show her some of the oldest and most famous parts of Stockholm. They walked throughout Gamla Stan, and Oliver pointed to a cathedral in medieval style amid the Royal Palace. A Swedish guard stood at attention near an arched doorway. They talked about his job, and he shared engrossing stories of his more fascinating closed cases—even the hard ones, though he left out graphic details. It was a perfect, cloudless day. Quiet alleys and pedestrians and flower shops littered their wanderings.

She told him about her mother. The words spilled out easily after an accumulation of the loss of the necklace and her homesickness. She told him how much she'd resented Rowan, but it had become too exhausting to carry it around forever. She told him about the first and only conversation she'd had with her father after that terrible Christmas evening. Her father had tried to help mend their relationship, but neither Lucia nor Rowan wanted to speak or repair. Oliver listened as their feet took them from neighborhood to neighborhood.

Lucia told him about other things, too. About her love for New York and Simon and Adeline. About the colors of the city in autumn. She told him about the echoed, reverent halls of the Met and her jogs through Central Park. She told him summer in the city was her favorite season despite the humidity. She told him about the jazz players from NYU who would often play in Washington Square Park. The city was her kitchen, her living room, her library. Her home.

By her third day in Stockholm, Oliver had resumed work. That morning, she woke up in his bed alone. She pushed herself up to her elbows and squinted at the sunlight coming in through the curtains. For breakfast, she made sweet porridge and a cup of coffee from his French press. She felt as if she was living in a snow globe, a miniature world in which nothing outside of it could touch her. Sipping her coffee slowly, she stretched her legs out on an empty chair with an ease she'd never allowed herself in New York. After messaging both Simon and Adeline that she was safe in Stockholm, both expressed relief, but neither asked about her mother's necklace.

When evening came, daylight would turn into dusky pink and dark stains of blue in the sky. At night, they would lose themselves to each other. Sex with Oliver was like a fever dream. After they'd satiated themselves, they talked for hours before falling asleep. Outside his bedroom window, Stockholm would descend into twilight, a city glowing like a cathedral of lights. The warm tenor of his voice soothed her, and she would close her eyes to listen. On her second-to-last evening in Stockholm, he walked through the front door after work and found her sitting in the main room. He came to sit on the armchair of the sofa. She placed a book of short stories in her lap, his eyes intent and proprietary above her. His smile was soft, dangerous.

"It feels like you've been here," he said.

"What do you mean?" asked Lucia.

Oliver tucked a strand of hair behind her ear as his eyes searched hers. "My sheets always smell like you." His fingers grazed her chin. "Like jasmine and fresh air."

***

The morning she knew she was leaving, Lucia woke early. Oliver was working part of the day, and she welcomed the solitude.

Finally, she dared to read the letter from her mother. She pulled the envelope from her suitcase, as intact and unopened as it was when she first received it in New York.

In the quiet of the flat, the letter brought about a tense anticipation in her chest. Unfolding the paper, her mother's neat handwriting on the page swam into her vision:

> *To my Starling darling,*
>
> *Since my cancer diagnosis, everyone who knows is afraid. Even the doctors. I'm not afraid of death, but with very little time ahead of me, I am terrified of what I've left behind.*
>
> *At first, I thought that we'd be able to get past Christmas all those years ago. I didn't mean for you to overhear me, but I convinced myself that my honesty was doing you a favor. Truth is an anchor, but I learned that it can be a weapon, too. You heard me in my greatest moment of weakness, and I've agonized over the fact that I am—despite all I've accomplished in life—the*

villain in this story. Mine and yours.

Language is a trap, Lucia. There were so many words I could not find to say to you after that night. The version of myself who said I didn't want to be a mother is a version of myself I don't understand anymore. I was so angry. I think I've always been. But what I've carried has nothing to do with you. I wanted recognition of my resentment. You have held me to a different standard as a mother than you ever did for your father. He had been granted leeway for the weeks and days we were without him as he flew around the world, and sometimes, it was lonely. I did the best I could, but it seems I got it wrong. Because you needed a mother, and instead, you got me.

My career in collecting rare pieces of history has taught me that women have been expected to live in service of the needs of everyone except themselves. We become invisible this way. Even though I chose to become pregnant, I refused to give in to what I believed was the doom of motherhood. By trying to avoid this pitfall, I fulfilled my own prophecy. If only I had received the complicated offering of motherhood as both a gift and a transformation. Your father has begged me to tell you I'd reached hospice stage, but how can I trust forgiveness under these conditions? And how could I force that on you? Apologies only relieve the guilty. We both know this. I think I deserve to be remembered as you last witnessed me. That is my punishment.

I'm leaving my jade necklace for you to either keep or donate, the choice is yours. But I give it to you with hope that it will accomplish what I could not with words; I'd found the necklace while pregnant with you, when the world seemed full of hope and possibilities, which is why I kept it all these years. Like a good luck charm. It was always going to be yours.

When I said I never wanted to be a mother, what I really meant was I didn't want to keep bearing the burden of disappointing you. I could always see it in your eyes. I had become the coldness of my own mother without realizing it. Everyone says they want to be remembered after they die, but what they really mean is they want their sins forgotten. I won't ask to be absolved, but know that I'm miserably, terribly sorry. I didn't love you the way you needed, but I do love you so much, Lucia. It took dying to realize the best part of me, this legacy I strived for, wasn't in a long marriage or an award-winning career but a daughter. And not just any daughter, but you, who somehow managed to survive me.

Rowan

Lucia sobbed and sobbed, covering her face with her hands. The paper pressed into her breastbone as she bowled over, as if in prayer. The letter was agony, and it was anguish. A wail she'd tried to stop since Rowan's death was swiftly on her lips. She'd waited so long to hear these words from her mother, but it was an embrocation weeks, months, years too late. The letter wasn't a storm brought to shore.

It was something far more difficult.

All the years she'd mourned her mother, even while she'd been alive, had been misery. Here at Lucia's feet was a wave of her own despair, the finale of her resentment and sorrow and hope. Rowan had been imperfect, but Lucia wished she'd understood sooner that her mother's sharpness wasn't only pointed at the world, but also herself. Lucia vowed then not to forget Rowan's faults but to stop holding them over her own life like a threat. It was up to her now to decide how she wanted to carry on. Here, finally, she might bring herself to a place of forgiveness she'd never imagined; not quite punishment, not quite absolution. It was bigger than that, and it felt like being hurtled like a comet through space, spiraling through the galaxy, leaving only love and heartache for her mother in its wake.

CHAPTER FORTY

Lucia had calmed down from crying by the time Oliver returned to the flat. The eternal sun of Sweden came in through the kitchen windows, splaying out on the wood floor.

With a calm reassurance, she knew something had changed in her this trip. She was ready to go home. Home was people. Home was Simon and Adeline. And her father. And the sounds of New York City.

As she packed, Oliver prepared their last meal together. She dreaded what she was about to do, hated the way she felt she had to do it. Her life was an ocean away and it was calling to her. They were both adults; they knew what this was, right? Could they let each other go when the time came?

She zipped her luggage closed and placed it on the floor. She took a nostalgic inventory of his room: a nightstand of books, a basket of laundry, a throw blanket draped across a chair in the corner. Everything was neat and in its place. When she walked into the kitchen, he scooped pickled herring into a small bowl. A Swedish pop song played on low from a Bluetooth speaker in the living room.

Is this how it was always supposed to be? This remembrance, this deep comfort?

"It's nearly ready," he said, leaning over to give her a quick kiss before turning off the stove.

"Oliver."

He heard it then, in her voice. He set the pan down on a different burner and turned.

"I leave tonight," said Lucia. She could tell he noticed her careful, cautious tone.

"This entire week has been wonderful," she said. "Really wonderful. But I leave tonight for New York. When I leave, I think we should ... just let this be as it is."

"You don't want this to continue," he said slowly, a contemplative expression as he sought to clarify what she was saying. "Or to even see each other again?" His hands rested on the marble countertop, a bit of hair falling across his brow. Lucia held back an urge to brush it off his forehead.

"I ... I don't think that's a good idea, Oliver," said Lucia. She turned away, unable to look in the eye of her own heartbreak. Her guilt was a bell tolling in her chest cavity. "I mean ... what did we think was going to happen? We knew I was leaving."

"I knew what I was hoping might happen," said Oliver, his voice gruff.

"And what was that?" She turned to him before she could stop herself from wanting to know.

"To be close to you," he said, reaching for her hands. "Being around you feels natural, Lucia. You're so rational about the things that don't matter and so willing to pursue at any cost the things that do. Being around you has felt ... " he searched for the words. "I couldn't stay away no matter the consequences."

"We have to be realistic," Lucia pulled from him, denying herself the thrill of what he was saying. Her arms hung heavy at her side. "Our lives are an ocean apart."

"So you want to go back, and you don't want me to convince you otherwise," said Oliver softly. His mouth had begun to lower into a sad smile.

"I fell apart after my mother died," Lucia's voice broke. She pressed the palm of her hand against the spilling tears on her cheeks. "I didn't want to face it because I wasn't sure how everything could keep going. But it has. Being back in New York without thinking of what I'm leaving behind is the way I need to move on. I *have* to."

"I understand." Oliver's voice was taut with emotion as he gently placed his arms around her. Her solace in a dark and lonely storm. "I understand, love."

***

She had taken a taxi to the airport instead of Oliver dropping her off. Her eyes had stung as she'd kissed him goodbye in his flat. Leaving him was already hard enough. Would it have been easier if she let him visit her in New York so they could continue the affection they'd started? But what would that mean? Long-distance emails, long-distance plane rides, missing each other? How do you build a relationship across an entire ocean?

It was a leap of faith she wished she could rationalize.

As she stepped onto a moving walkway two gates away from hers, her name came over the loudspeaker.

"Lucia Starling, please check in at the desk at gate twenty four. Lucia Starling, please check in at gate twenty four."

Puzzled, she hastened her pace. She had already checked the monitors and confirmed her flight would be leaving on time. Groaning, she wondered if she would be bumped from the flight being overbooked. It had happened before, and the prospect of several hours of delay made her feel more miserable.

She brought her suitcase upright on its wheels at the airline desk. "Hi, I'm Lucia. This is my flight. Is there something wrong with my ticket?"

The attendant at the desk gave a warm smile. "Yes, Ms. Starling. Follow me, please. We have upgraded your ticket to first class."

Lucia was taken aback as the woman gestured to the jet bridge. Mutely, Lucia grabbed the handle of her suitcase and followed her. The attendant briefly flashed her badge and a paper ticket to the gate agent.

By the time they made it to the open door of the plane, she knew. The instant her father's captain hat came into view, she threw her arms around his shoulders in relief. He hugged her back with a squeeze. With hands on her shoulders, he looked at her.

"There now, if you cry the entire flight, I'll have to place you in the emergency row of the cabin," he teased. "That's where we stick the difficult passengers."

"You would never," said Lucia, a mix of sniffing and laughing.

"That's what you think." His eyes crinkled at the edges. She hugged him again, and his co-pilot in the cockpit gave her a polite smile and wave as he prepared for take off. She motioned her head toward her father.

"Hi. I belong to this guy."

"G'day. Nice to meet ya, I'm Byron. Your father mentioned he was having family on this flight," he said. Byron returned to a map in his hand.

"So that's why you asked about my flight." Lucia turned to her father.

"I tried to put you on standby, but as it turns out, there was one empty seat in first class. Do you know anyone who wants to take it?"

"Is it terribly uncool if I raise my hand and say *me*?" asked Lucia with wide eyes.

"It's all yours," said her father. He handed her the paper ticket the attendant had before. "Passengers will be boarding soon. Go ahead and take your seat." When she nodded, he started to say, "And remember—"

"I know, I know, there's no crying in first class."

By the time the plane made its way down the long runway, she held a soda water in her hand. She hadn't bothered choosing a movie or watching the flight map at take off. Pulling the privacy divider closed, Lucia only wanted to watch the clouds. A blanket lay across her lap, and she leaned against the frame of the plane. The engine rumbled beneath her as memories of Oliver bloomed in her mind.

The surprise of seeing him on the train.

His eyes across a dinner table in Amsterdam.

His tenderness the first time he kissed her.

Holding hands as they walked into his mother's house.

The way he wanted to know about her mother. Not because he had to but because he wanted to understand Lucia better.

She'd left home thinking two weeks would be an escape. As if a different country would buy her peace. She'd been desperate for it. But leaving for Italy had been impulsive, and she'd been given something else in return. What had happened in Rome, Amsterdam, and Stockholm had led her to rediscover the thing she had forgotten or had been on her way to forgetting: the triumph of being alive. The gift of it. The tragedy of surviving her mother. Her father flying the plane to take her home to New York. An unknowable future. She felt more prepared now than when she'd left.

You can never return to the time before.

In itself, she felt that it deserved its own recognition and reverence.

The plane took off, leaving land. The future felt uncertain, and his words tethered her to a world that felt laden with hope and mourning. She missed the moon over New York.

The plane floated silently through the clouds, offering a view that made her wonder if heaven existed in the same dimension as the one she was in.

An ache pressed itself inside her chest, clarity and desire smashing together. *Love*, Oliver had called her. *Love*.

Love, love, love, love.

Chapter Forty-One

"How's your dad doing?" inquired Adeline as she handed her son Theo a crayon at their table in the restaurant.

"He's doing well. We're going to see a movie tomorrow."

Lucia sat across from Adeline and her mother, Corinne. Simon was running late to meet them, but they had ordered coffees to sip in the meantime. They were having brunch in Midtown. A summer rainstorm splashed yellow cabs outside the window.

In the weeks since her return home, Lucia desperately missed Oliver. She missed him every single day with a longing that had surprised her. He hadn't contacted her, just as she'd asked, but part of her wished she hadn't shut the door so firmly between them. It had been harder to ease back into the city and the life waiting for her here when her thoughts were a country away.

"What movie are you going to see?" asked Corinne. Her thick and curly hair was in an afro style, perfectly matching her gold leaf earrings and dark, wide lashes.

"The new one about the ship in space," said Lucia as her phone pinged. "It's him. He needs me to come by. Apparently, there's some mail for me?"

"I wonder what it is," something flickered on Corinne's face, but just then, Simon came through the door of the restaurant. She waved a hand expectantly over the rectangular table. "Well, we've been waiting."

"Good God, has anyone told you you're *gorgeous* today?" Simon leaned in to hug Corrine. She gave him a kiss on the cheek, leaving a faint smudge of red from her lipstick.

"You smell like a wet dog," chirped Theo.

"*You* smell like a wet dog," said Simon as he sat, affectionately tapping Theo's nose. "Did you already start without me?" he turned to the three of them.

"I have nothing exciting to add," replied Lucia dryly, "but any longer, and your impatient audience was going to eat me alive."

"Well," Simon rubbed his palms together, building up the suspense. "I wanted to wait until we were all together, but after careful consideration of the, *ahem*, various laws I broke in favor of helping *you* in Rome," a sidelong look at Lucia, "I should tell you that I now have a boyfriend."

"That is *not* where I thought this was going," Adeline gasped.

"As it turns out, Lorenzo helping catch that woman with a red notice by Interpol for *multiple* burglaries—"

"—*and* money laundering across multiple countries," added Lucia.

"—got him a promotion," Simon finished with a nod. "And said promotion led to a job opportunity in New York. He got here last week, and he's staying with me until he finds his own apartment."

"Let's be real, Lorenzo's never moving out," Adeline tossed her head with a laugh.

"Let it also be said," interjected Lucia, looking at Simon, "I'll never be able to thank you both enough. I know it all worked out okay, but I owe you both for what you did to help me."

"There's nothing I love more than someone being indebted to me," joked Simon, giving her a wink. "Also, at risk of you trying to chase down someone else across Europe, ask someone else next time."

Lucia reached across the table for his hands with a sober expression. "I vow to never, ever again follow anyone across Europe because of a stolen heirloom."

Simon squeezed her hand across the table with a sweet smile. Adeline and Corrine reached over with their hands, grasping onto Simon and Lucia.

"Is this like the Three Musketeers?" Theo asked innocently as he placed his small hand on the top of the pile.

They howled with laughter. A twinge of heartache still echoed, but Lucia tucked it away. Even without Oliver and without the necklace, here were the people she loved and who loved her; in this city, this one tragic and beautifully bewitching life.

***

After the bill was paid, they stood chatting on the sidewalk in front of the restaurant. The rain had finally relented, and the pigeons and the garbage truck had resumed their familiar noise.

Lucia texted her dad. *I'll be there in 15 minutes.*

Adeline put her own phone in her bag. "On your way to your dad's house?"

"I am," said Lucia.

"I'll go with you," said Adeline, handing Theo's toy to Corinne, who nodded. Corinne gave Lucia a kiss on her cheek, color blooming from her lips.

"Have you left some red on me?" asked Lucia.

"Barely," Corinne gave her a wink. "But it suits you."

Adeline looped her arm through Lucia's, and they walked together. As they were on her dad's block, Lucia reached into her bag for her phone. Adeline stopped her, pointing.

"What is it?" asked Lucia. Shifting her attention to the end of the block, she let out an audible gasp.

There he stood, like something out of a dream, a wish, a memory. Oliver.

Slowly, she walked toward him, a cautious expression on his face. With dark jeans and his hair sweeping his forehead, he was exactly as she remembered. Tall, lean, eyes dark and stormy, as if she was the first and last woman on earth he wanted to drink in. The weeks since they'd seen each other collapsed into no time at all.

"Hi, Lucia," said Oliver.

Lucia had never seen him appear remotely nervous before. Not once when she'd pulled him off the train in Amsterdam or when he'd wrestled the gun from Mia. But here he was.

"Is there an express train from Sweden to New York I don't know about?"

His lip curled, and he crossed his arms in amusement. Delight slowly melted from one feeling into another as each second passed. She was overwhelmed by the sight of him.

"You really got on a plane," said Lucia in awe and confusion. "An international flight to come here? Why?"

He held her gaze, unflinching. "For this," said Oliver. He pulled a black velvet box from his pocket.

Her heart beat wildly, afraid. Afraid to hope, afraid to imagine. She didn't have to be afraid for long because the moment he opened the box to face her, she touched it with her fingertips.

It was real.

"How did you ... "

She gingerly lifted her mother's necklace out of the box and clasped it around her neck. Lucia couldn't find the words. It was cool to the touch, just as she remembered.

"How the hell did you find this?" she cried. "How did you track down the buyer Mia sold it to?"

"I am," a curved smile grew on his lips, "occasionally useful."

"I suspect you're somehow behind this?" declared Lucia as she turned to Adeline, pointing at her.

"He contacted me about two weeks ago," Adeline laughed as she pulled Lucia into a hug. "He told me who he was, his credentials, and that he'd found the necklace. Between Simon and myself, we worked together to time his arrival today. Well, your dad, too, since he got Oliver the flight."

All of the details folded together like a seamless deck of shuffled cards. Shock left her speechless.

"So you're Adeline," said Oliver with an outstretched hand. She watched them officially meet. Her best friend and the man she loved. It was like staring down a kaleidoscope, her universe colliding in a flash pan of color. Lucia thought her heart was going to burst out of her chest with so much unspeakable, unfamiliar joy.

"How did you find it?"

"Samaran, mostly. He and I visited Mia a few times until she finally gave the information we needed with a small bargain of reduced time. Now that she's in prison, she is very willing to give up everyone else. Turns out, the buyer Mia sold the necklace to was wanted for another case in Belgium. The minute I had it in my hands, I wanted to see you."

Her eyes were pools of tears, threatening to spill.

"There's more," added Oliver.

Her head leaned forward, her hands on the necklace. "More than this? More than you?"

"Yes. The woman who hired Samaran wants to speak with you about putting it on permanent display at a museum. She has close connections throughout most of France and England. If you should want to. The choice is, of course, all yours."

All she could manage was to continue staring at him, taking the sight of him in. "I'll think about it," said Lucia, reeling. "So ...you're here. In New York City—for how long?"

"I'll be seeing you later," called out Adeline from halfway down the block. Lucia hadn't even realized her friend was nearly gone. She smiled as Adeline blew a kiss.

It was only Lucia and Oliver. A summer breeze picked up, rustling the tree leaves above them. New York swirled around her, but all she could see was Oliver.

Lucia stepped closer, one hand on the necklace. Her fingers traced the shape of the jade that was so familiar to her. Oliver watched her, his eyes clear and steady. Lucia closed the space between them, reaching for him. They both held on.

EPILOGUE

Monte Carlo, One year later␣␣

In a harbor, blue and green boats rocked lightly to the rhythm of the current. Docked vessels swayed, rippling splashes of seawater against the bow. Luxury yachts slowed their course to enter calm waters.

On rose bushes, bird feathers and dragonflies slowly descended. Striped white and blue umbrellas dotted the beach. Tourists flocked to the water in their swimsuits, plush beach towels and slip shoes discarded in the sand. The coastline was reminiscent of a different time, with muted tones of blue and ivory. French flags waved in the breeze. Near the beach stood a line of boutique hotels flanked by cypress trees. Off Avenue Princesses Grace, one villa in particular was frequented by tourists and locals alike. In the museum, a new exhibit of rare and precious jewelry from around the world was on display. Honeymooners and friends came and went up the curved steps leading inside. Parquet flooring gleamed as a runway for women of wealth who strolled through, wearing wide-brimmed sun hats. Soft voices and chatter echoed off the floors.

In a white, pleated dress, Lucia stood in front of one single exhibit, eyes brimming. Glasses of champagne floated around on silver trays for the exhibition opening. She heard her name and turned to find Samaran.

"It's ... spectacular. I don't know how to thank you," said Lucia.

"It's good to see you again," said Oliver, smiling to give Samaran a solid handshake.

"I'm not the one to thank, though I have brought the woman who will gladly accept it." He gestured to a stunning woman in her sixties who walked up to the small group. Her hair was neatly tucked in at the collar of her navy blouse and wide-leg silk trousers. Despite her stoic expression, the woman's gray eyes sparkled.

"I'm Lucia, and this is my husband, Oliver," said Lucia. "It's nice to finally meet you in person. Samaran, of course, has said wonderful things about you."

"Cecilia," she said coolly, but the upturned smile at the corner gave her away. "Don't listen to anything he says."

Lucia bit back her own smile. "When he mentioned you were a benefactor to a museum that could put the necklace on permanent display, I was so—"

"Gratitude is not necessary in this instance," said Cecilia, her shoulders square. "Besides. Samaran so infrequently asks me for anything."

"It feels like a miracle to see it here. She ... my mother would have loved it." Lucia swiveled toward the necklace encased in glass on a high marble stand. Rays of light slanted across the floor. A small crowd gathered around the display, leaning in for a closer view.

"Samaran will tell you I'm not a sentimental woman," said Cecilia with a wave of her hand. "How long are you here?"

"We'll leave for New York this weekend," replied Lucia.

"I hope you'll join me for lunch tomorrow, then."

"Ah, well. Alright," said Lucia with a quick nod. "Tomorrow will be lovely."

"Tomorrow it is," said Cecilia. "Perhaps we can discuss some possible business opportunities together." She grabbed a delicate glass of champagne off a passing tray.

"Oh?" asked Lucia.

"From what I hear, you are very capable of finding rare pieces, which seems to run in your family."

"I'm not sure about any kind of career in locating jewelry, if that's what you mean—"

"Let's chat more tomorrow," said Cecelia as she adjusted her Italian leather handbag. With a wave to someone behind Lucia, she said, "I'll have Samaran connect us through my assistant. I see someone I must speak with now. Please enjoy the rest of the exhibit."

The invisible scent of sandalwood followed as Cecilia departed. The three of them turned to see her air kiss the cheeks of a sophisticated older couple. Lucia turned to Oliver and Samaran, amazed.

"She's ... " said Oliver.

"Just as I expected from my phone calls with her," said Lucia with a light chuckle. "I admire her tenacity."

"She's a force," added Samaran, a twinge of awe in his voice.

Lucia attempted to cover her smile with her champagne glass.

"Seems like you've got a possible career in locating rare artifacts," Oliver reached for her hand. "Should you quit your job at the UN?"

"In this economy, not likely," Lucia smirked.

Oliver brought her hand to his lips, kissing her knuckles. A gold wedding band flashed in the light. Together, the three of them stood facing the exhibit. A woman in her fifties traced a finger along the words on the plaque. She read it aloud to a young girl who appeared to be her daughter.

"It was only recently donated to the museum in honor of a woman named Rowan Starling," recited the woman.

The significance of the plaque had nearly brought Lucia to tears when she'd seen it. On its display, the necklace was in the brightest room of the space, the poignancy of the event resurrecting her grief. Her past, her present, and her future crashed into her like the sea colliding with the shoreline. Noticing her, the woman gave Lucia a gentle gaze.

"Are you here for this exhibit, too?"

"I am," said Lucia lightly. "I donated this piece for the exhibit."

"It's an extraordinary necklace," commented the woman as she studied it behind the glass. "I've never seen anything like it."

"Thank you." Lucia's eyes glinted, luminous green orbs shining through a fog of mourning she was still surviving. Her mouth formed a soft smile, a whisper of who she was and where she came from. "It belonged to my mother."

BONUS CHAPTER

Check out this free *Starling Darling* bonus chapter!
It's called *The Moon Over New York,* and takes place two years after
Starling Darling. Download *The Moon Over New York* at the QR
code.

As an author, reviews are appreciated and even better, contribute to
a book's success so I can publish more books! Please consider leaving
a review on Goodreads.

ONE NIGHT IN WARSAW

Amara Rhodes is in danger.

Alone in the dead of night, she arrives in France with sleeves covered in blood, seeking refuge in a cottage on the verge of falling apart. In her possession is an encrypted hard drive with information a major human trafficking organization would kill for. She runs from everything she loves; a legal career in MI6, her flat in London, and a relationship shrouded in secrecy.

But from the moment she steps foot in the small French town, both the animals and locals begin to take a keen interest in her. When a man in town mentions her by name, it becomes a race against time to get the hard drive into safe hands.

One Night in Warsaw is both an epic love story and Amara's journey of realizing what she's not willing to lose in order to survive: her humanity.

BOOK CLUB GUIDE

This reading group guide for *Starling Darling* includes discussion questions and ideas to enhance your book club. The questions are intended to delve into topics and varied perspectives from the story.

1. In the first flashback, Lucia loses track of her mother at Coney Island. How did you interpret Rowan's reaction? Do you think this scene was a pivotal marker that, had it gone differently, could have changed the outcome of their relationship?

2. A focus on the story also revolves around Lucia's relationships with her friends. What do you think is the importance of found family for Lucia?

3. Lucia decides to book a train ticket even without her passport; in what way can you relate to her desire to maintain forward momentum to recover a stolen personal object?

4. In Chapter 15, we see Victor's experience of grief through the eyes of Oliver. Why do you think this is a powerful point of view to tell this particular perspective?

5. An added layer of the story is an examination of trauma and its unintended consequences. Given the home life Victor experienced growing up, what connections do you make between his home life and the crimes he commits?

6. While Victor and Lucia have opposing personalities, they have both experienced loss and neglect of a parent. In what ways do you think they overlap? In what ways do they differ?

7. When we think about place as a main character, how does each city/country impact Lucia and her memories of Rowan? Can we draw an arc of progression of where Lucia begins in New York to how she feels when she returns?

8. The heart of this story centers around grief and a mother wound. What is a quote from the book that you think captures this feeling for Lucia most acutely?

TRAVEL GUIDE TO ROME

72 hours in the eternal city

Day one

St. Peter's Basilica

Reserve your tickets weeks in advance. A way to also enjoy the experience of Vatican city is to sit along the curved steps and people watch.

Dinner at Nativa

A vegan restaurant in the hilly Aurelio quarter. I'm convinced you can't have a bad meal in Rome. In the land of carbohydrates, meat and sugar, this dinner will convince you anything they make is delicious..

Piazza Navona at night

Walk Piazza Navona at night (the place where Lucia, Oliver and Victor meet!). There are several marble statues on travertine crafted in this famous square in central Rome. The various masterpieces throughout the piazza are artworks in Baroque style by respected artists Boromini and Bernini, who are known to have had a contentious rivalry. If you are like me and enjoy the niche interest of rivalries in art history, I highly recommend *The Genius in the Design: Bernin, Borromini and the rivalry that transformed Rome.*

Day two

The Journey: *Fontana di Trevi → Via delle Muratte → Via del Corso → Piazza Venezia → Via dei Fori Imperiali → Colosseum*

Trevi Fountain

Located in the Trevi area, the fountain was built in the 18th century and depicts a sea scene. Even at 8:00am, it *still* isn't quite early enough to beat major crowds. If I could go back, I would have been there at sunrise. If you find evening more enjoyable, the midnight hour makes for an equally quiet, stunning time to admire the fountain.

South on Via del Corso

Their simple but pleasurable limone flavor is a great treat to enjoy while you spend time popping into nearby shops.

Colosseum

An interesting dimension of traveling in the 21st century juxtaposed with ancient architecture is that you have a lot of information at hand. An audio tour gives extra context and appreciation of how and when the elliptical amphitheater was built.

Lunch at La Nuova Piazzetta

A classic lunch: pasta with mussels. In the pursuit of flavor and delicious food, Rome really has it all..

Day three

The Journey: *Piazza del Popolo → Via di Ripetta →Via Metastasio → Via Maddalena*

Piazza del Popolo

(Translated literally, it means the 'People's Square') Sometimes there's s lively music performance you can enjoy, but full disclosure: a bit of research will reveal the square actually has a bit of a dark history related to public executions. Places like Rome with so much history means learning about the past, and it's not always perfect!

Pantheon

The former temple is breathtaking in person. The city recently began charging a small $5 fee for entry. The supplemental tourism charge can better fund the capital's infrastructure, which is not able to keep up with the influx of visitors each year.

Dinner at Il Margutta

The oldest vegetarian restaurant in Rome was an elevated food experience at its finest and most niche.

About the Author

Erica Vipond is the author of slow burn romantic thrillers that will keep you guessing. She has a B.A. in English and a love for studying languages. When not writing, you can find her binge watching Kdramas, baking sweets, and reading Dramione fanfiction. *Starling Darling* is her debut novel.

Join for giveaways, bonus chapters & new releases:
www.EricaVipond.com
Find her on Instagram
@EricaVipondAuthor

ACKNOWLEDGEMENTS

I wrote this book three months into the Covid-19 pandemic, and it became a life raft while my world (and everyone else's) transformed into something very different than planned. What began as a love letter to my life in New York City became a much longer dedication to the other places I adore in real life: Rome, Amsterdam and Sweden. Thank you to the following people:

Ashley, for seeing the early draft and understanding the story I was trying to tell. You have never doubted my dreams to become an author and I'm so grateful.

To every beta reader who took time out of their lives to read the book and help me improve it: Thank you Marina, Eva Claire, and Blake.

Abby, whose watchful, empathetic eye over my personal evolution has been critical for me these past 10 years.

Lauren, who painted the incredible cover art for my debut book. Two dreams came true at once!

Miranda, who polished this book, and banished every misused punctuation mark. You were the final, most important component to making sure this book became real.

Elisa, world's greatest godmother, who inspired the brilliant facets of Linnea, and parts of the story which took place in Sweden. You taught me how much good there is in the world when we look for it.

To the following women who either read the first draft, every newsletter and always believed in my dream to publish a book, I'm so lucky I don't have only one amazing friend but rather, an entire tier of you: Dar, Stephanie, Casie, Ashley, Virva, and Kristin.

To every reader who deeply understands that nothing is as fierce a teacher as a mother wound: I see you.

To J. Writing book husbands from my imagination is fun, but I'll choose you every time.